DRUM

OF HOPE

JAY CROWLEY

ALSO BY JAY CROWLEY

Maggie
Not Worthy – Story of Revenge
Opal
Cabin in the Meadow
Ship in the Desert
A Selection of My Short Stories
Laura
Natalie's Adventures – Middle Grade
A Gift from Nate – A Story of A Double Lung
Transplant

ANTHOLOGIES

Other Realms I & II
I Heard it On the Radio
13 Bites III & IV
Plan 559 from Outer Space MK II & III
559 Ways to Die
Free For All
The Collapsar Directive
Relationship Add-Vice
Christmas Lites VII, VIII & IX
Tales of the Southwest

Email: jaycrowleybooks@gmail.com

Facebook: Jay Crowley-Sweet Dreams Books

Amazon:https://www.amazon.com/JayCrowley

For updates on new stories and more information on the author or books; visit www.sweetdreamsbooks.com

DEDICATION

This story gives you a little history with the rebuilding of the Sutro Tunnel and a little mystery. I am sure you will learn something from this story.

I want to thank all the people who make writing a story for the readers possible. First, a draft, then individuals read, correct, or tear it apart, and then the rewrites. Josie Leeds is the individual who spends her time, correcting work. Couldn't do it without her...Thank you so much.

There is more information about the author in the following book coming out on Amazon May 1, 2020. It is an honor to be included.

Chapter One

Angelica opened her eyes to semi-darkness; she was bound and gagged. She felt something scurry across her feet. She tried to screech inside the gag and jumped in pain. *What is that? Was it a rat?* She tried to sit up, but every bone in her body hurt, her heart was beating fast. Her hands were tied in front of her. Her legs were bound, plus being gagged. It took tremendous effort will all the pain and cold, to have her hands pull the gag partially out of her mouth. She managed to get the gag out enough to scream. Her mouth tasted funny like copper, from the material, *had they chloroform her? Would it do any good to scream? Would anybody hear me? I doubt it.* She thought as her teeth began to chatter. She wondered how long she had lain in the cold?

She was not only cold, but damp. Angelica could see light at the end of the tunnel or whatever place she was laying in. The cold was so bitter, as she only had a bikini on her small hundred and ten-pound body. Her teeth wouldn't stop chattering.

Angelica felt blessed; she was still alive; they hadn't killed her. She thought, *how long will I live? Will I freeze to death? Or will someone find me? Or will they come back to finish me off?*

Angelica attempted to sit up, but with her legs bound, she tried to untie the rope, but no avail. All she could do was scoot, but it hurt too much to move. *I have to try. I can't die here!* She started scooting, but after just a few feet, she was exhausted from the pain and the cold. *I am going to die...* she thought as she passed out.

Chapter Two

A few years back, Maggie, a grandmother, decided to take up writing. She felt it would keep the brain active. She is now an independent published author. This means she works for herself.

Maggie lives in Jacks's Valley, with her husband, Pete, and Yazoo, her six-year-old black Labrador. Maggie and Yazoo hop in the Jeep with her partner in crime, Nan, to wander around Nevada, taking pictures. The pictures give added information for the different stories Maggie writes. She writes mainly for magazines, though she has a few novels out.

Most recently, Maggie had been contacted by some old friends who are members of a group trying to restore the old town of Sutro and the Sutro Tunnel. The site located outside of Dayton, Nevada, not far from Six Mile Canyon. Friends of the Sutro Tunnel are hoping to preserve this area as a historical site for tourists to visit.

The mine, at its time, took ten years to build. So to house the miners and staff that worked on the tunnel, the town of Sutro was built. In the sixties, artists started to live in Sutro, and it stayed an artist colony into the seventies and eighties. Nonetheless, today, no one lives there, and the town is deteriorating.

Maggie used to visit a quaint bar there, even though she hadn't been to Sutro for years, so she didn't know if it was still standing. With the group trying to restore the Tunnel, Maggie contacted a Nevada magazine and thought this would make a great story, and the editor liked the idea.

Maggie did a lot of research on the Sutro Tunnel, plus growing up in Virginia City. The Sutro Tunnel started in the town of Sutro outside Dayton. The Tunnel ends at the Savage mine up in Virginia City. It missed its mark by about ten feet. Not bad considering the time and their tools.

A little history, back in 1863, thirty-three-year-old Adolph Sutro believed that a tunnel excavated intersecting with the lower levels of the

Comstock mines would drain out the hot water. The tunnel would allow the mines to dig deeper shafts for gold.

Sutro was quite a promoter and sold stock to other miners for this adventure. The miners paid to move the ore and also have the mine water drained through the tunnel.

The idea was to construct this tunnel so it would remove the hot water from the deep mines to a pond that flows to the Carson River. Sutro also had a mine, and he operated in nearby Dayton. He pushed the plan through Nevada Legislation to obtain a mandate for his Sutro Tunnel Company to excavate an approximate four-mile tunnel from Dayton to Virginia City.

It took almost ten years to build at the cost of around five million dollars, and by the time it was completed, the ore in the Comstock lode was declining, plus most of the big mines were deeper than his tunnel. Sutro, however, was able to sell his stock and made a profit of about one million dollars before moving to San Francisco and became its mayor. While the Mayor of San Francisco he also built the famous Sutro Baths.

According to historians, the Tunnel was used in the great winter of 1889 to haul food and supplies to Virginia City, as there was so much snow the Virginia & Truckee railroad couldn't run. Virginia City had over six feet of snow.

Ranchers were losing stock because the temperature dropped to -42 in some places, colder in others. Again, according to historians, the winter of 1889-1890 has no parallel in Nevada history until the winter of 1948, the Elko Hay Lift, and the big snowstorm of Virginia City in 1969, but those are another story.

Today the Sutro Tunnel entrance and the remaining buildings sit roughly on twenty-eight acres, and water still drains from the tunnel from some of the mines in Virginia City. The pond is still there to collect it.

Maggie, Nan, and their dogs planned on going to Sutro to take pictures today. Maggie had received permission from the Sutro Tunnel Company to visit the site as, at this time, it's gated.

"Hey Hon, I will be gone for a few hours, there is lunch in the refrig if you get hungry," yelled Maggie to Pete, her husband of forty-five years. He was in the bedroom watching the TV.

She heard Pete mumbled something as she went out the door.

Nan and Bill Morgan lived only a few streets away, so it just took a few minutes to arrive at Nan's house. Maggie pulled up in Nan's driveway and tooted the horn. Nan came running out with her jacket, a picnic basket, and her dog, Shep. Shep is part Border Collie and Sheltie. Nan always came prepared with food and drink.

Maggie retired two years ago from working with the Reno Aces Baseball team. Nan retired from Harley Davidson Finance Company in Carson City last year.

Nan and Maggie both are in their late sixties. However, Nan is thirty-pound thinner, with short blonde/gray hair. They have been the best of friends for years.

Yazoo and Shep were the best of friends for at least five years. The dogs even have playdates. Yazoo started howling like he always does when he sees Shep, with his tail hitting the seat.

"Be patient, Yazoo, Shep is coming," cooed Maggie.

"Maggie, this is going to be an interesting day. The weather is great, and you should get some great pictures. Did you bring the drone?" chattered Nan.

"No drone. I hope I never see that thing again after using it on the airmail arrows and horse poachers," laughed Maggie. "I am looking forward to visiting Sutro, as it has been years since I've been out that way."

"Same here. The last time I was there... must've been about twenty years ago," stated Nan.

Dayton is a little over twenty miles from Jacks's Valley where they lived, so the trip went fast.

Maggie explains, "It is hard to believe that in 1961, Dayton won fame as a setting for John Huston's film, 'The Misfits,' the last movie appearances with Clark Gable and Marilyn Monroe. It was about wild horses being round up."

"Yeah, I think I had heard this story before," laugh Nan, "the last time you told it we got shot at."

Maggie never skipped a beat and went on to say, "In the 1990s, Dayton experienced phenomenal growth as residential development expanding on the east side of the Carson River, with the Arnold Palmer golf course that was built."

Taking a deep breath, she continues to rattle on, "all of Nevada felt the growth occurrence. Las Vegas was having thirty-five hundred people a month move in, Reno about one thousand a month. Then the recession hit, and the bottom fell out everywhere in the State."

Nan continued the conversation, "I understand the historic part of Dayton is within a small Comstock Historic District. I understand it features main street, the monumental Odeon Hall, and a charming local museum located in an 1865 schoolhouse---I understand it is the oldest in Nevada in its original location. We should go visit the district, might make an interesting story."

Maggie thought *as she drove, maybe I should do a story about Dayton. It's a town with an interesting past. It was the stopover on the way to California in the 1800s. Also was named after John Day, a surveyor who laid out the small town. Hmm, have to think about it.*

"Dayton also claims the designation of being Nevada's oldest settlement, a title disputed by the residents of Genoa, which sits at the base of the Sierra Nevada's, west of Carson City," stated Nan. It is about five miles from where they live.

"The Mormon Fort and the Genoa Bar were founded in 1860. So I think Genoa, is the oldest," laughed Maggie.

Seeing Maggie hadn't been to Sutro in years, she was surprised that there was a housing subdivision built right up to the private land.

"Wow, has this all changed. I didn't know so many people lived in Dayton," claimed Maggie.

"Yeah, I remember when this was way out of town," chimed Nan.

"Remember when people would say, who would want to live in Dayton?" laughed Maggie.

Maggie, with her GPS, located the dirt road to Sutro. There was a gate across the road, but the Company had given her a key. She laughed, though, as trucks had driven around the gate.

They pulled up as close as they could to the Tunnel entrance, so they only had to walk a hundred yards or so.

"Well, let the adventure begin," as Maggie grabbed her camera. Nan took her phone.

Chapter Three

As they hopped out of the Jeep, the dogs started to run. Maggie yelled at Yazoo, "come, stay close." Shep came back with Yazoo. Maggie didn't know if rattlesnakes were around. She checked her gun, a nine-shot 22 pistol. It was in her holster on her hip, just in case she needed to use it.

They started walking up to the Tunnel. The ground was wet from the winter weather and the runoff from the Tunnel to the pond. As they got closer to the entrance of the shaft, Yazoo started barking. Maggie saw the Tunnel gate was partially open.

"What's wrong, boy?" as Yazoo seldom barks. "Is there an animal in there?"

Nan stopped and listened, "I think I hear something, sounds like a whimper. Maybe an animal is in there, and it's stuck."

Maggie took her gun out of her holster, just in case, it was a bear or a coyote. Carefully they approach the entrance to the Tunnel. Maggie wondered why the iron gate which covered the entrance was unlocked. When she got closer, she looked at the lock. "Nan, it looks like the chain been cut." *Must be vandals,* she thought. "Darn, I don't have a flashlight," complained Maggie.

Nan said, "I have my phone, always come prepared," she laughed, and shined the light inside the tunnel as they walked in. They both held on to the dogs firmly.

"There is something over there by the tracks, over behind that cart," stated Maggie.

They both said in unison, "What the devil, it's a body!" As they ran over to it with the dogs.

Nan bent down and felt the young girl's neck as the girl whimpered, "there is a weak pulse. Thank goodness she's still alive, but barely".

Even in the semi-darkness, they could see the girl was severely beaten. Nan got on her phone and was about to call 911 when a voice stopped her, "No! No police, they will kill me for sure," said the voice in a low whisper.

"You need help. We need to move you out of here and get you help".

The girl whispered, "I am tied up, could you help me, and maybe I can walk out."

"Well, I have to see about that. Do you feel like anything broken?" asked Nan.

"No, I don't feel anything, but pain, I'm just so cold," she whispered with teeth chattering.
With that, Maggie took out her knife from her belt and cut the bonds, and removed the gag from around her neck, and it smelled putrid, she shoved it in her back pocket. Together they tried to get the girl up without hurting her anymore. They got her up on her feet. However, she was so weak.

The girl hardly weights anything, so between Maggie and Nan putting her between them to hold her up so they could walk her out. The hardest part was walking out of the tunnel, which was only maybe ten yards to the entrance.

The girl winced in pain, but never cried out. Once out, Maggie ran to the jeep to retrieve a blanket, which she quickly wrapped the young girl, as they had her sit on a log in the sun. The dogs stay close to the young girl. The poor child couldn't stop shivering.

Maggie commented, "I wish we had something hot for you to drink. I am sorry."

The girl said nothing as she wrapped the blanket tighter around her. Maggie and Nan had lots of questions. Who is she? What was the young girl doing in the Tunnel? How did she get so severely beaten? They both had grandchildren older than this girl. They just sat there with her and waited.

Nan retrieved some water and first aid kit from the jeep. She gave her some water and used the first aid kit to clean up some of her cuts, and the girl said nothing.

Without the child watching, Maggie took a couple of pictures of her. Even beaten, she was a beautiful girl with long black hair, brown slanted eyes, and an olive complexion. She could be native American, Spanish, or maybe Basque. Either way, Maggie thought *she someone's daughter*.

Some color started coming back into the girl's face, and she finally quit chattering from being so cold. What is your name?" asked Nan.

The girl looked at them both for a minute, hesitated, then finally said, "Angelica."

"What a beautiful name for a beautiful girl," asserted Maggie.

A little smile came across Angelica's face, and she said, "I don't think I look so good right now." They smiled back at her.

"Angelica, I have lots of questions. Do you mind answering?" asked Maggie.

"I will answer what I can."

"Do your parents live around here?" asked Nan.

"No."

"Where do they live?" asked Maggie.

No answer, she just shook her head no.

"Did you run away from home?" queried Maggie.

Angelica shook her head, yes. Maggie thought this is not getting us anywhere.

"Are you hungry?" asked Nan as she brought up some sandwiches from the Jeep.

"Yes." Angelica took a sandwich. Maggie and Nan ate half a sandwich too. All of them sitting in the sun. Yazoo stayed closed to Angelicia like he senses something was wrong. Maggie threw a treat to the dogs. Nan lit up a cigarette.

"Do you know that is not good for you?" stated Angelica.

Nan coughed, caught off guard, "Yeah, but I only smoke a few. Maggie just shrugged and smiled. *Like saying I told you so...*

Maggie thought, *I don't know what to do with this girl? A crime has been committed, but she doesn't want the authorities. We need to find out what happened.*

Chapter Four

A good hour passed as they sat in the sun, trying to warm up the girl. At least she had stopped shivering. Maggie did walk around, taking some pictures, and making notes. She also calls the Sutro Tunnel Company to let them know about the broken chain on the tunnel gate. However, she didn't mention the girl.

"Angelica, do you feel like getting in the jeep?" questioned Maggie.

"I think so, it will be slow, but I think I can do it," whispered Angelica. They got up and, like before, with one on each side, helped her walk to the Jeep.

When they got there, Maggie asked, "Angelicia is it okay to place my hands on your rear to help you in?"

She shook her head, okay, and it worked. The girl was strong. She didn't cry or shout out, getting in the Jeep had to hurt. Her bruises were everywhere. It looks like whoever had taken the belt or the whip to her was very angry. Yazoo sat next to her, licking her hand.

"Angelica, I think you have found a friend. I'll be taking you to my house so that you can get a bath, and we can properly dress your wounds. Is that okay?"

"Yes. Thank you."

Maggie thought *the girl was very polite, so she had proper training from her parents. Again, I am inclined to believe she is Native American, but she could be Portuguese or Italian. It doesn't matter. I just wonder how am I going to help her?*

The girl, so young, wrapped tightly in the blanket, was finally warm, and she fell asleep on the way home.

Maggie whispered to Nan, "we need to ask the girls at the quilting club for help."

"I think you are right, This girl is going to need some counseling, I believe Betty has some counseling experience or knows some people who could help her," Nan said quietly.

When Maggie dropped Nan and Shep off at their house, Angelica woke up. "We will be at my home in a few minutes, did you get a little rest?" inquired Maggie.

"Yes. I feel safe with you."

"Thank you. I will do whatever I can to help you. But you must also help us," replied Maggie.

Maggie pulled into the garage and noticed Pete's car was gone, which was probably good. Maggie and Yazoo jumped out of the jeep. Then she came around to help Angelica out. It took some effort, but again the girl never cried. Maggie thought *she is one tough cookie.*

Maggie walked her to the guest room, which formerly was her daughter's room—mostly used by her granddaughter now. Looking in the closet, Maggie found some clothes she thought would fit Angelica. They might be a little outdated, but they were clean.

"Try these on after your bath. They should fit."

"Thank you for your kindness," Angelicia whispered with tears in her eyes.

"Anytime, are you up to a shower to get cleaned up? Or do you want to lay down for a while?" inquired Maggie.

Hesitantly, she replied, "I think the warm water would feel good."

 Well, here is a towel and a washcloth. Everything else is in the bathroom."

Around twenty minutes later, Angelica came out of the bathroom, fully dressed, in a pair of jeans, a tie-dye T-shirt, and barefooted. Her hair shinned, she looked beautiful except for cuts and bruises. Maggie thought, *how could anyone do this to a child?*

"Looks like you need some shoes," laughed Maggie as she went looking for a pair.

When she returned with a pair of flip flops, Maggie said, "sit here and let me dress your wounds, though most look like welts. What monster took a belt or whip to you like this?"

No answer.

Yazoo came and put his head in Angelica's lap. "That's okay. You will learn to trust again." as Maggie put salve on the open wounds.

Chapter Five

Several days passed, Maggie hardly knew Angelca was in the house, she stayed in her room, sleeping most of the time. Yazoo barely left her side, as he had truly bonded with the young girl.

Maggie was letting her recover from the beating. Nonetheless, even weak, Angelica did offer to help with the meals and the dishes.

Maggie and Nan had decided to leave Angelica alone until she felt comfortable with them, as this child had gone through a lot. Pete hadn't said much. He just accepted, they had a house guest with a problem. But knowing his wife, she would tell him about it when the time was right. He did wonder about the girl's injuries. The welts were going away, but the bruises from them would take weeks.

Tuesday afternoon, Maggie was working on the computer, writing her draft about the Sutro Tunnel, when Angelica came in and sat down.

Yazoo, who had been lying in his dog bed, came over for love from the girl.

"Hi, how are you doing? Are you hungry?" asked Maggie.

"No. I am fine. Thank you. Do you have time to talk?" the girl asked.

"By all means. What is going on?

"I think you need to know what kind of person you have under your roof. I am not a nice person," whispered the girl with a distressed look on her face.

"Tell me all about it, and let me see if I agree with you," smiled Maggie patting the girl on the shoulder.

Angelica got a sad look on her face, "About nine months ago when I was fifteen. I ran away from home. I have two older brothers and younger twin sisters. We live on a small farm, and we all have lots of chores. Maggie thought, *five children, wow.*

"Where was this?" Interrupted Maggie.

"I don't want to say yet," and continued with her story. "I felt my parents were too strict. We couldn't even afford a cell phone! Besides taking care of my younger siblings, I worked two days a week as a dishwasher in a local restaurant. The job helped me to earn money for my clothes and school things. Plus, I had a demanding boyfriend. So you can see how busy my life had become."

Angelia stopped for a moment, then continued. "I knew we were poor, but somehow my parents always had food on the table. My dad works 4-10's in the mine, and Mom works long hours as a waitress." Maggie listened, never asking any questions, but thinking, *teenagers. Everything is a crisis.*

"You see how I look? Well, I got teased at school because of my looks. I never fitted in. Plus, most of my clothes came from the thrift store. Finally, I couldn't take it anymore. I figure there had to more to life than this. I had talked to a couple of girls online that lived in Reno, and they told me about good-paying jobs and fun things to do."

Angelica got up and started pacing, as she had tears in her eyes, but proceeded to tell her story.

"I bought a ticket for the bus to Reno. I had enough money saved to stay at a cheap motel for a day or two, hoping to find a job. Which I did, I found a job at Taco Bell, but I wouldn't get paid for ten days. I knew I didn't have enough money for the motel, and I didn't want to sleep on the street. Through other kids, I heard about the Eddy House for homeless kids and spent some time there. They were great. I met some super people, and all was going okay."

She pauses for a minute before she continued. "I did have occasional sex with men for money to survive, only three. They also bought me food and clothes." Angelica buried her head in her hands. "I was a paid hooker."

She paused a minute before she started in again, "after several months on my own. I met this

32

girl, Rebecca, who was a few years older than me. She told me about this guy who had a beautiful house, with a swimming pool and he took in kids to help them out.

I went with her to meet him. His name was Brent, and he was kind, not old, maybe in his late thirties, and he walked with a little limp. He was so nice to me, invited me to stay at his place, at no cost. He even had me quit my job, saying that he would take care of me because he was falling in love with me." Angelica was crying now.

Angelica froze a little, when Maggie hugged her, then relaxed. Maggie thought, *whatever this child has been through, must have been hell...*

"I became his lover; life was wonderful. I was free to drink and smoke pot. He had about twenty girls staying at his place. I never saw them much. But the best part was he was in love with me... or so I thought." Again, she got up and started walking around the office.

Maggie could tell she needed to take a break and poured her a cup of coffee. Angelica took a couple of swigs and started in again. "Last week, I celebrated my sixteen birthday. Brent gave me a beautiful necklace. I was walking on air.

A few days after that, he called maybe ten of us girls into his office. Several of us had been in the heated swimming pool when we went to the meeting in the family room. That is why you found me in a swimming suit.

Brent said in a very firm voice, "you now owe me for my generosity." He further went on to say. "He wanted us to go out into the night and earn five hundred dollars each doing tricks." I was aghast.

That is when I made the fatal mistake of asking, "what if I don't make five hundred dollars?"

He yelled at Frank, one of his security men, "Bring her to me, hogtied and gagged." Everyone in the room said nothing, as they were scared.

After tieing me up, Frank dropped me on the floor in front of Brent.

Brent then whispered to me, "I hate to do this, but you are disposable," taking off his belt he started whipping me, yelling this is what you'll get if you don't earn five hundred dollars."

"He beat me until I guess I passed out, and you found me in the tunnel." Tears were flowing down her young face. Maggie grabbed some tissue and gave them to her with a big hug.

"They left me for dead, and if they find out I am not, they will kill me because I know too much. I know who he is and where he lives. I think he would also kill the other girls to get rid of the evidence."

Maggie said, with tears in her eyes, "you have so much, too much on your young shoulders. I will take out that no good bas... I can't say the name. Trust me. I took out a cartel poaching horses. I can catch a vile sex trafficker."

Angelica just looked at Maggie with a puzzled stare, "You would do that for me?"

Maggie hugged her tight, "Darn right, and Nan will help. Plus, there is a group of us that will help kick his butt. We may have to tell the police."

I am afraid for the other girls if we call the cops," stated Angelica. "Maybe later, but not now."

"Okay, for now, we can talk about it Wednesday night at the quilting club."

Angelica smiled and felt relieved that she had told Maggie the truth. Maggie, on the other hand, her mind was racing. *How do we catch this slimeball, especially when Angelica doesn't want the authorities involved?*

Chapter Six

With Angelica's permission, she called Nan and asked her to come over, as they had work to do. Within minutes Nan was there. "What's happening?"

Maggie and Angelica filled her in. Nan was beside herself. "How could anybody do that? It is a crime called sexual seduction. He needs to be put in jail," as she ranted on.

Maggie said, "He is clever. He waited until she turned sixteen to put her to work so that they couldn't get any of the John's for child rape." Maggie was furious.

When Nan calmed down, They decided to talk to the quilting group tomorrow night for help.

Every Wednesday night was quilting night from six-thirty to nine. The group had been meeting for several years. Maggie always looked forward to seeing her friends.

The quilting club meets at the Fabric Chics in Gardnerville, and their group is called the 'Wild Stitchers.' Maggie could make one quilt to the other ladies three. It was an inside joke.

When Nan, Angelica, and Maggie came into the meeting that night. Everyone looked at Angelica, mainly at her bruises.

"Gals, this is Angelica, and she needs our help," stated Maggie. Maggie then proceeded to introduce the club to her.

"Nan, who you know, does beautiful woodwork for fun, plus make quilts to sell. She is a smart-butt and smokes," laugh Maggie,

Everyone laughed.

"Beth is the baby of the bunch at forty-two, she still had children at home as well as owning and operating this fabulous fabric store. Beth, besides being a young, lean, hard-working quilting machine momma with that long blond hair and beautiful blue eyes. She is also the teacher of the group," snickered Maggie.

Beth blushed. "Thank you, lady, for the kind remarks."

"Mary Normandy-Sorenson is very soft-spoken, so you have to listen to what she says... sometimes we don't." Everyone laughed. "She works at the Douglas County Sheriff's Department, in the Detective Division. She loves making quilted pillows so she can give them to family or friends for gifts. Mary is a newlywed. We think she the quietest one of the group because she the tiniest and in her early sixties." Mary made a face with a smily frown at Maggie.

"Betty Santos is the other part of our group." Betty still works at an insurance company, even though she is in her early sixties. She will never retire." Again, everyone laughed. "However, She's cute. Maybe she is a little robust who dyes her hair blond to keep her young. Betty has lots of grandbabies. She loves to makes baby or couch blanket type quilts, which she also sells at craft fairs."

Beth piped up, "and of course you know Maggie, she is our trouble maker, a little fluffy with short brown hair. However, if you need a pit bull, she's it." Maggie stuck her tongue out, and everybody laughed, including Angelica.

Everyone said, "hi." Then they asked Maggie what she needed. Maggie proceeded to tell the group about the sex trafficker. The group was appalled that someone would do this to a young girl, Mary thought, *She is only sixteen.* They all thought *we have grandchildren older than her.* Beth, though, *my daughter is almost her age.*

Angelica sat very quiet and looked at her hands, this was unnerving, she didn't know these people, but they wanted to help her, and she could be putting them all in danger.

Maggie proceeded to tell them that, "Angelia could be in danger because she knows too much. She is afraid that the other girls at the house, where she lived, could be in danger too. Because of that, she doesn't want the police involved yet."

Everyone shook their heads in understanding.

Betty was first to comment, "Angelica, you need to have some counseling. I know a Shaman who does excellent work."

Angelica looked at her, funny, "Why a Shaman? In fact, what is a Shaman?"

"A person who can help and won't go to the authorities," replied Betty. Angelica then understood.

Mary stated, "I will have to stay out of this. I can nose around. But I have to be careful as I am hiding a crime." Everyone shook their head in agreement, as they understood Mary's position.

Angelica hadn't been a great help, as she wouldn't tell them much about the sex trafficker, except his name was Brent, no last name. There was no certainty that this was correct. He could have given her a false name.

After much discussion, they decided that Betty would take Angelicia to the Shaman on Saturday. Tomorrow Nan and Maggie would check the Sutro area to see if anyone noticed a vehicle coming or going about the time Angelica had been dumped.

Mary would see if she could find any information on a Brent, which was like a needle in a haystack.

Beth said, "I am no help, except for moral support."

After all the planning tonight for Angelica was done, Maggie was ready to start a new project.

Even though she may be slow compared to everyone else, she did finish a king-size log cabin quilt for her daughter last year.

So far this year, Maggie had completed an applique wall hanging of an owl in a tree, which hangs in her hall. Tonight, she is going to start working on a crazy quilt lap blanket.

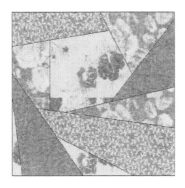

For each block was approximately 13" x 13", Beth showed Maggie how to cut a muslin foundation. Then choose one of these five-sided patterns in the middle of the block: middle one or middle two and so forth. The pieces were taped together. She had to be careful not to tape it on the sewing lines, or it could gunk up your needle when she put them together.

Beth said, "Maggie, you will need to make twelve blocks."

So Maggie figures, one block a meeting will take her four months to complete, then she must add the stuffing and backing. So maybe five months total. She thought, *a lot faster than the king-size quilt* as she pours herself a glass of wine.

Chapter Seven

The next morning, Nan, Maggie, and the dogs took a ride back to Dayton. They had left Angelica with Pete.

"Maybe someone around here must have seen something out of the ordinary that day," quipped Maggie.

"True, someone had to bring in the child and dump her," smirked Nan.

They drove around the subdivision close to Sutro entrance, looking for someone, who may have seen something. It seems like everybody was gone, guess they're at work. Finally, on the last street across from the Sutro dirt road, they saw a garage door open. Maggie drove up and stopped.

"Hi," she said to the old man who started to sit in his chair in the garage. A walker was beside him.

"Hi." He said back.

Maggie and Nan got out of the Jeep and walked up to the man. Maggie put out her hand,

"Hi, I am Maggie, and this is Nan. Do you sit out here much?"

"Hi, I'm Bud Freer," as he shook her hand. "And yes, I sit out here, weather permitting, every day about this time. However, I also watch whatever is going on from my front room. I am like the Block Watch person, to make sure all is ok, while people are at work."

"Wow, that sounds like you take on a lot of responsibility. I hope you can help us, as we have a few questions about any going on at Sutro. Do you think you could help?" Asked Maggie.

"Yep. Like your jeep was up there a few days back. Let me see as he grabbed a note pad. It was last Tuesday at 8:30 am."

"Wow, you are right. We went up to take pictures as I am doing a story for a Nevada tourist magazine," responded Maggie.

Bud when on to further say, "you were up there about three hours. Two of you went up with dogs, but three people came back with the dogs, and your Nevada license plate is BLT 003."

46

Nan replied, "you are certainly observant. Did you notice anyone before us going up there?"

"Yep. A red Ford Pickup with a black tonneau cover on the bed, not quite sure of the age, but fairly new, so probably 2015. Two men. They didn't stay long, maybe fifteen minutes."

"What time of day did all this happen?" Queried Maggie.

Checking his notes, "Monday, around ten-thirty p.m., I was in the house watching the television, waiting for the news," the old man said quietly. "I figured they were going up to drink, but they didn't stay long enough."

"Thank you so much. You have been a big help. You didn't by chance, catch their license plate.?"

"Sure did, not all of it though seeing it was dark. Don't see so well at night. It was a Nevada personal plate, HVAN, there were two more letters at the end, that I didn't catch."

"Thank you so much for all your help. You don't know how much you have helped. It may save lives," expressed Nan.

Bud blossomed with the kind remarks. "I have nothing to do, with Edna gone, so sitting out here watching life go by is my joy."

"Do you have children, Bud?" Asked Maggie.

"Yes, but they live in different states and have lives of their own. Meals on Wheels comes once a day and brings me food. I can drive, just not much anymore. Life is good, I have my Sadie for company."

Neither of them had noticed the old golden retriever lying behind Bud on a doggie bed. Who now looked at them.

"Beautiful dog. Thank you again for your help," whispered Maggie.

"May I asked what is going on?" asked Bud.

"We wish we knew, but I will let you know when we get this all figured out," sputtered Nan.

"May I give you my phone number in case you see the truck again or anything that looks unusual," as Maggie gave him her number.

The girls got back in the Jeep and waved goodbye to Bud. "Boy, did we get lucky. But we need to bring him a home-cooked meal and desserts," commented Maggie.

"Agreed, he is a sweet old man."

"Now, to get this info to Mary so that she can run the plate."

Chapter Eight

They took the license plate information to Mary at the Sheriff's office. Mary was busy filing reports.

"Hi Mary," said both of them.

"Found some interesting information, can you help? However, I don't want to put you in an uncomfortable situation," stated Maggie.

Mary gave them a discouraging look, but said, "what is it?"

"We have a partial license plate for a red Ford pickup, around 2015, maybe newer," sputtered Nan.

"This may be the vehicle that dumped Angelica. We are not sure, but it meets the timeline. It this uncomfortable for you?" Again asked Maggie.

"What do you have?" whispered Mary.

"Nevada personal plate HVAN with two more letters at the end, but we don't have those," sighed Nan.

"I will see what I can do. This may be easy. Personal plates are easier to track," said Mary.

Maggie said gently, "thank you so much. We truly appreciate the information. Let me know what you find out."

"I did learn something. I have it right here on the daily blotter, two of our deputies arrested a couple of young girls for soliciting, they were from Reno. According to the blotter, they looked to be eighteen years old or better. They told the officers pretty much what Angelica had said about the guy, they lived with at 22689 Cottage Parkway, Sparks, but no name for him," shared Mary.

"Can you give me their first names so that I can tell Angelicia? Also, I will ask her about the address," stated Maggie.

Mary bowed her head, "I can only give you their first names, and we are not sure they are correct, as they had little identification on them. Tanya and Cleo, and you didn't hear it from me."

"Thanks again," they both said and shuffled out the door.

Betty unbeknown to her quilting friends practices a mixture of Paganism and Native American beliefs about Mother Earth. She's a sole practitioner, as she doesn't belong to any circle. She likes to practice her beliefs on her own in her way.

Even though it's late Spring almost Summer, of the four seasons, Spring is Betty's favorite time a year. It is when Mother Earth rejuvenates. Ostara is a time of rebirth; it is a time of awaking. It is a time of equal parts light and dark. Ostara is the Goddess of Spring. To honor her, Betty buried an egg by the big old elm tree in her front yard. The egg helps with the rebirth of nature and gives nutrients to the tree. The egg is the perfect representation of this aspect of the season.

Saturday morning, Betty went to Maggie's house to pick up Angelica. She's taking Angelica to see Walking Eagle, who she hopes will help her find peace. The child can't blame herself for what has happened to her. Kids don't always think things through. If anyone can help her find peace, it will be Walking Eagle. Hopefully, with the use of the sweat lodge. Betty explained to Angelica what would happen when she entered the sweat lodge.

Angelica was apprehensive about going into the sweat lodge. Nonetheless, she knew Betty wanted to help but wasn't sure how all of this was going to help her.

When they arrived at the Shaman's house, Betty explained, "Walking Eagle is a spiritual Shaman. He practices a variety of earth-based faiths."

Walking Eagle is only sixty, but he looks a lot older with his long white hair and weathered skin. He's been a Shaman for thirty-plus years. Walking Eagle has a positive attitude about life and spirits. Betty felt he's perfect for helping Angelica.

Walking Eagle had built an enclosed area in the middle of his three-acre Johnson Lane property.

It's a beautiful ten by ten-foot structure that allowed his circle to meet outdoors, yet protect them from the elements when necessary.

Betty tells Angelica that "a Pagan sweat lodge isn't as formal as a Native American sweat lodge, but they all seek the same answers."

Betty feels Angelica needs solutions to understand what has happened to her and find peace.

Walking Eagle guided them into the sweat lodge. The bonfire was already lit outside the lodge with the stones, getting hot. After Walking Eagle carefully brought the heated stones into the lodge with deer antlers and placed them in the center pit. He started meditating, and when he closed his meditation, he invited them into the lodge.

Walking Eagle had them take a place on the ground, then anointed them with oil on their foreheads, and smudge them with sage. The sweet smoke and smell helped to calm Angelica's nerves.

Walking Eagle began the actual ritual by walking the boundaries of the lodge with the burning sage. A brief invocation to the spirits of the four elements, air, fire, water, and earth, were offered at each of the directional shrines.

After a few minutes, Angelica and Betty started to sweat as Walking Eagle chanted. At first, Angelica was scared, then peace settled in. She knew she wasn't a bad person and started to cry. Betty embraced her. After a bit, Walking Eagle opens the flap on the sweat lodge and walked out. Betty and Angelica followed.

"You have a good heart, Angelica. Things will get better. Trust Betty, Maggie, and Nan. They will help you find your way. Also, to help you find your way, tomorrow, we will make your Drum of Hope."

"What is that?" asked Angelica.

"The Drum of Hope is part of your soul, you will see. Tomorrow", as he walked away from them.

Betty drove Angelica back to Maggie's house. Angelica felt relaxed and was at peace for the first time in a long time. She loved the smell of sage.

"Thank you so much for taking me to meet Walking Eagle," stated Angelica.

"Not a problem. See you tomorrow at one," replied Betty as she drove off.

Chapter Nine

Maggie felt it was time to tell Pete what was going on. She walked into his office and asked, "Do you have a minute?"

"Always for you," he said with a smile.

Maggie stuck her tongue out at him as she sat down in one of the office chairs and proceeded to tell him what was going on.

Pete was pacing the office by the time she finished. "Maggie, I understand you want to help this child, it makes me furious that some adult would treat her this way. But have you thought of danger we are in if they find her here?

Plus, you are not Jessica Fletcher from Murder She Wrote. Remember last year, when they shot at our house, because of your investigations of horse poachers." He repeated, "now you have put us all in danger again with this situation. These people play for keeps. Look at what they did to this girl!"

"What am I supposed to do, leave her on the street, making a living on her back?" she snarled.

"Of course not. Take her to the Sheriff's Office. Let them handle this. That is their job," snapped Pete.

"I can't do that."

"Can't or won't."

Maggie got up to leave the office saying, "I guess I figured you wouldn't support me on this, and now I see you won't. Don't worry. I will make sure your butt is safe," as she stormed out fuming.

Pete mumbled something about her being the most stubborn woman he had ever met and slammed the office door.

Maggie could still hear him throwing things in the office, as she left the house with Yazoo. She thought, *what if this was our daughter? Or granddaughter?*

The next afternoon, Betty picked up Angelica, and they drove over to Walking Eagle's place. Today they were making her Drum of Hope. Angelica didn't have a clue what it was but was looking forward to making it. She liked Betty and Walking Eagle. When they arrived, Walking Eagle had everything laid out on his dining room table. There were wooden circles, deer hide, and deer gut for strings.

He chanted over the materials before they began. He showed Angelica how to stretch the hide over the wooden frame, chanting while she was doing it. He asked her to chant with him, which she did. For the first time in her young life, she felt completely relaxed and had hope.

Tears fell on her drum as she made it, chanting all the time. In a little over an hour, she had completed her drum. She touched the hide with a slap, and it made a beautiful sound. Then she painted a deer on it and made a drum stick. The drum had a piece of her soul in it, and she felt it. There was hope. She was not a failure. Angelica knew she would survive.

On the drive home, her mind wandered. *I got to help the other girls getaway from Brent. She was afraid he would do to them what he did to her.*

As she got out of the car, she hugged Betty, "Thank you so much for introducing me to Walking Eagle. I love my drum; it will be my savior."

Chapter Ten

Angelica came bouncing in the house with her drum. She found Maggie in the office and said excitedly," I am ready to help you get Brent."

"Wow, let's do it," said Maggie. "Let me call Nan."

Nan was there in ten minutes with red puffy eyes.

Maggie said," Okay, what is going on? I can tell you have been crying."

"Nothing, this is more important,' sighed Nan.

"Cut out being a martyr, what is going on?" questioned Maggie.

"Bill has cancer," cried Nan, holding her hands to her face.

Both women hugged her. "Tell us exactly what is happening."

"Things will be okay. It is the best kind of cancer to get, its prostate cancer. Everything will be fine. It just caught me off guard. I see my husband as indestructible. He might have to go through radiation for a few treatments, but all will be great."

"I understand if I learned that Pete had cancer. Darn, it would be so scary. There is no cure for that darn disease. Bill is in my prayers," sighed Maggie.

Angelica gave Nan a big hug, "I understand, my Mom had breast cancer, it scared all us kids, but thank goodness, so far she is still in remission, that was over three years ago. I don't want to lose my Mom."

They talked a little more about what they could do about Bill's disease and how to make Nan feel better. Maggie opened a bottle of wine and a coke for Angelica. Angelica brought out her Drum of Hope and started chanting to help Bill. It had a calming effect on Nan, plus the wine.

As the three of them sat in the office, two of them drinking wine, they started making a plan. Angelica opened up, saying, "Brent's last name is Stevens. I know that is the truth as I saw a letter addressed to him. He or Fred always got the mail, but one day he left it lying in the bedroom, and I saw it. The address of the house is 22689 Cottage Parkway, Sparks. It is a fancy home, three stories with a large gate."

"We could send the police over, but I am not sure they would do anything without seeing Angelica," ranted Nan. "Yet, we don't want to put you or anybody else in any danger." She said, looking at Angelica.

"I agree," replied Maggie. "We need to catch him in the act, as it were. The sad part is it only takes a few seconds to kidnap a child, or coerce a woman with violence or a boy and put them in the sex trade – but years to prosecute the trafficker."

"How was he to collect the money?" Asked Nan.

"That I don't know as he beat me up before getting to that part. I imagine when the girls come home, but he may have a pickup place... I don't know," and Angelicia started to cry in frustration.

Both Nan and Maggie embraced her. Maggie stated, "Don't worry, we will figure this out. Let's sit on it for a couple of days. We should hear something from Mary. Talk about Mary, darn, I almost forgot. She said the Sheriff's office arrested two girls, Cleo and Tanya, does that sound familiar?"

"Yes, Cleo is a blond girl, and the other has dark hair like me. They are older, maybe 18-19. Can they catch Brent because of them?"

"That I do not know, but we will find out," said Nan.

Angelica stated what she wanted to do, "I want to call Brent and meet him."

"Definitely not," shouted Nan

After much discussion, it was decided not to do anything until they all meet on Wednesday. Angelica wasn't sure this was a good idea but went along with their decision.

"Changing the subject, how did the drum class go?" asked Maggie.

Angelica just beamed, "it was awesome. My drum makes a beautiful sound. Walking Eagle says it has part of my soul in it. It is my Drum of Hope."

Everybody hugged and smiled to see Angelica happy for the first time. She was a beautiful girl with a beautiful smile.

Monday morning, Maggie's house phone rang, "Hello."

"Hi Maggie, this is Bud Meyer. You said to call you if I saw anything, well, I saw that truck. It came by Saturday. I left a message for you with some man for you to call me. When I hadn't heard from you, I decided to call again."

I am thankful that you did as I didn't get the message." Maggie was furious with Pete. "What did they do?"

"Well, they drove up to Sutro, was there only a few minutes, then they came racing out, going like heck. Surprised they didn't hit anyone," stated Bud.

Maggie thought *they came to get the body, and it was gone. Nothing in the news, so now they suspect she is alive.* "Thank you, Bud, that gives us a heads up. Be careful, and if they come back, don't let them see you, they are dangerous.

Bud, all excited, "this is better than TV. I will be careful. I also have a gun and know how to use it."

"Bud, for a few days, you might want to watch the goings-on from the inside of your house," warned Maggie.

"Thank you for the warning, and I just might do that," replied Bud.

They both said goodbye. After Maggie hung up the phone, she went looking for Pete.

Maggie called Nan and told her what was going on, and Angelica was sitting next to her.

"Angelica, you are safe here. They don't know you are with us, so don't worry."

"I can't believe they came back, what if you hadn't found me?" She was in tears.

"Well, we did, so don't think about what 'if' You will be okay," said Maggie firmly, but not believing it herself.

Angelica and Yazoo ran into her room, and she started playing her drum.

Wednesday came fast. The three of them went off to the quilting club meeting. Maggie was looking forward to getting another block done. But mainly they were curious about what Mary had found out.

Everyone came in, all said, "hi." Everyone decided that Angelica would also join in, doing a project. Beth felt Angelicia should make a table runner. The wine flowed, and the conversation began.

"Mary, what did you find out?" asked Nan.

The truck belongs to a Fred Jones, The full plate is HVANDY. It is 2015 pickup, and the address is..." Mary had to look at a piece of paper, "22689 Cottage Parkway, Sparks."

"That is Brent's place," stammered Angelica.

"So we have come full circle, " said Maggie.

They all looked at each other, what do they do now? "What about the two girls arrested, what did you find out?" questioned Maggie.

"From what I understand, their lawyer made bail as soon as possible, and they were released. There is a court date set, but bet you they won't show," stated Mary.

"So we truly are back to square one," sighed Nan.

Maggie told them what Angelica wanted to do. "She wants to call Brent and meet him. Nan and I don't think that is a good idea, what do you guys think?"

Mary said. "I will ask one of the detectives about it. I know they are not excited about putting a child in danger. However, they know we need to catch these people."

Everyone agreed with hesitation and concern for Angelica. At nine, the class finished, and everyone started to leave. "I am not sure what to do next, guess we will wait to hear what Mary finds out," said Maggie, frustrated because everything was moving slow. Everyone shook their heads in agreeance.

Mary said, "I'll check with one of the detectives tomorrow to see what they recommend."

"That would be great, give me a call, when you find out,' stated Maggie.

Chapter Eleven

Thursday morning, "Angelica, I have a serious question for you," said Maggie. "Do you want to call your folks and tell them you are okay, I am sure they are worried about you. I know if my daughter were missing for months, I would be going nuts."

"I have thought about it, but not sure what I would say. I know I've hurt them, especially my Mom," replied Angelica quietly.

"The main thing to say is, you are okay, the rest will come easy," proposed Maggie.

After a few tears and an embrace, Angelica decided she would call her parents. She took Maggie's cell phone and went to the bedroom for privacy. A half an hour later, Angelica came out with red eyes from crying. However, she had a smile. *What a beautiful girl* thought, Maggie.

Angelica gave Maggie the cell phone, "Thank you," sighed Angelica before her an Yazoo went back to the bedroom.

Maggie didn't ask how the call went. She would wait for Angelica to talk to her. She knew it wouldn't happen right away. Maggie thought *I'll leave her alone and work on my Sutro story.* She went into her office to type it out. Maggie could hear Angelica playing her drum.

The History of the Sutro Tunnel
Maggie McDonald

In 1859 with the discovery of silver in the Comstock Lode, which was the first significant silver deposit discovery in the United States, numerous mines were opened.

One of the cities created during this boom was Virginia City. The City reached its peak of population in the mid-1860s, with an estimated 25,000 residents.

Virginia City, in its hay-day, had gas and sewer lines on A, B, and C street. A beautiful one hundred room International Hotel with an elevator, three theaters, and eight bars on C Street. Piper's Opera House was built on B Street. There were four churches scattered throughout the City as well as three daily newspapers. The town had three brothels located in the center of D Street, below the Bucket of Blood.

Many homes and buildings in Virginia City were made of brick. Some were made out of 2x12 wood, which went horizontal and vertical. This made the walls of the homes built out of 4x12's. These types of houses were built to withstand the brutal winter weather. Many of the homes were scattered throughout the whole side of Mount Davidson.

Nevada's winter weather was hard on the miners and their families. Snow could pile four to six feet high in a decent storm and stay for months. With each new snowstorm, more snow was added, making it almost impossible to trek off the mountain, even with snowshoes. There was a time when Virginia City had nine feet of snow at one time on the ground during winter. The snow could last until Spring

The lumber for the mines and homes came from Lake Tahoe about sixty miles away. First, the wood came by buckboard, then by rail on the Virginia and Truckee Railroad, commonly known to the settlers as the V & T Railroad. The much-needed rail

74

line was built in eighteen months with Chinese and Irish workers. Supplies and timbers were then shipped in from Lake Tahoe, and ore was shipped out to San Francisco by the railroad.

The V T was a standard gauge train that could handle the mountain in the winter. Drinking water for the City was flumed in from Marlette Lake about twenty miles away as the crow flies. Virginia City itself had lots of water. The problem being, not all of it was drinkable due to the mercury, arsenic, and cyanide from the mines.

Virginia City seemingly developed overnight on the eastern slopes of Mount Davidson, perched at a 6200-foot elevation. Within the town itself, mines dug intricate tunnels and shafts for silver and gold mining. They were woven in such a manner that they undermined the whole City. If an earthquake occurred, which happen now and then, a tunnel and sometimes part of a building would collapse or create a sinkhole.

The Comstock Lode discovery and the subsequent growth of Virginia City were unmatched in the history of any other precious metal discoveries. During Virginia City's peak, a vast amount of gold and silver were removed from the area mines and sent to California, as stated by rail. Notably, this gold and silver helped build San Francisco, California.

During this time, a gentleman by the name of Adolf Sutro, a middle-aged, educated individual, who was a civil engineer, lived in Virginia City. Being well known in the mining world. He envisioned in 1860 a drainage tunnel, which would allow access for deeper mineral exploration within the Comstock Lode. Mine flooding, clean air, and inadequate water or air pumps were inhibiting some of the exploration activities at that time. The water in some mines was scalding hot and had to be drained before the miners could work the claim. Not all mines had hot water, but most mines had water of some sort.

He received funding from various sources. Adolf called them "stockholders." Sutro also received Nevada Legislation approval to build the tunnel. He started construction of the Sutro Tunnel.

The tunnel started in Virginia City at the Savage Mine, emptying approximately four miles southeast near the town of Dayton and close to the Carson River. For its time, this was an extraordinary engineering feat.

They completed the tunnel on July 8, 1878, nine years after construction began. The tunnel ran 3.8 miles between Virginia City and Dayton at the cost of about five million dollars.

Adolph Sutro became the King of the Comstock because his tunnels drained three to four million gallons of water a day. He would rent the tunnel to mine owners at an average of $10,000 a day to haul their ore by mules, with "all money accumulated going to his stockholders."

However, Sutro saw in time that German air pumps were becoming available. The mines in the Comstock also were going even deeper than his drainage tunnel, plus the veins were diminishing in metal output.

Nonetheless, they still used the tunnel to haul ore and transportation for miners to the town of Sutro.

The mines' silver and gold output started to decline around 1878, which was about the time the tunnel was finished. The tunnel now didn't look so good as a moneymaking project.

Based on all of this information, he sold his shares before the conditions worsened further, he departed rich to San Francisco, California. He would later become the mayor of that great City. He also built the famous Sutro Baths.

Even with the decline of Virginia City's mines, mining remained a large part of Nevada's life and still does today.

As stated, due to the high elevation of Virginia City, the digging for the precious metals had to be deep. As the mines went deeper than the tunnel, it became rarely used. It was used to transport people and food, mainly during an emergency.

Today a portion of the tunnel is collapsing due to the ongoing drainage of water and lack of maintenance. However, the Sutro Tunnel continues to function as water still drains into the nearby pond.

There is a group trying to preserve Sutro as a historical site for tourists to visit. Can you imagine traveling the tunnel from Dayton to Virginia City, possibly being driven in a sled by mules?

If you are interested in supporting this cause of restoring the tunnel, contact Friends of the Sutro Tunnel. https://thesutrotunnel.org/

Maggie thought the story looked good, and she sent it off to the editor of the magazine. They would edit, send it back, and she would make the changes.

Now to concentrate on another story. Maggie was thinking about something around the Como Peak area. It used to be a mining town at one time, and it is located outside of Dayton. It seems there's a lot of history around Dayton.

However, for the time being, she needed to concentrate on Angelica's problem. They needed to catch Brent.

Chapter Twelve

Maggie yelled from the office at Angelica and Pete, "You hungry? I am going to fix some sandwiches." She heard positive remarks from both Pete and Angelica.

She went to the kitchen, making grilled ham and cheese sandwiches. A few minutes later, she hollers, "They're ready."

Everyone came walking in. Maggie and Pete haven't been talking much since the fight, and his lack of support hurt Maggie. He only spoke to her about the bare necessities. Maggie placed the plate of sandwiches on the table with a bag of chips and ice tea. The food went quickly. No one talked, just ate.

Angelica finally said, "After talking to my parents today, I told them if okay with you, I would stay here. I told Mom I wasn't quite ready to come home yet. My Mom wasn't happy about that. She said I'm needed at home, and everyone missed her. However, she was glad I called and that I was doing okay. I didn't tell them about Brent. No use in upsetting them about what kind of trouble I am in."

Pete glare across the table at Maggie. "You are more than welcome here," stated Maggie looking at her husband. "Pete, this could have been our daughter, or worse yet our granddaughter, think about it."

He got up quickly and started to leave the room, "I have," he said as he stormed out.

Angelica said, "I'm so sorry I'm causing this problem. I'll leave."

"Don't let him upset you. He gets this way. Shoot, he's a man," laughed Maggie. Angelica had a funny look on her face and was thinking, *and we have to solve this problem.*

The rest of the day was quiet. Angelica stayed in her room with Yazoo, playing her drum. Pete was in the office. Nan and Bill had gone to Fallon for vegetables. Maggie tried to read, but her mind was racing. *How do we catch this guy in the act?*

She got out her chalkboard and started in,

1 We know his name. Brent Stevens

2 We know where he lives. 22689 Cottage Parkway, Sparks.

3. We have the plate of the truck, which dumped Angelica.

4. We know the owner of the red ford pickup truck, Fred Jones. He lives at the same address as Brent

5. We know or think we know the names of two of his girls, Tanya and Cleo.

6. We have pictures of Angelica with her bruises. Also, I have the bandana. They used as a gag, *I forgot about that.*

One question Maggie had that perplexes her, on what she understood about sex trafficking. Women or girls can be shipped from city to city or state to state to provide specific services for men. Yet no one notices or reports this crime unless the girls are caught or rescued by the police.

From what little research she had done, since meeting Angelica, *it's stated that the sex industry is divided into two distinct classifications. Legal prostitution and trafficking. However, in Nevada.*

A girl over eighteen or a woman who works in a licensed house of prostitution does so on her own free will. Angelica, however, was being forced into prostitution, which is known as sex trafficking.

What am I missing here? I think a road trip is in store. Tomorrow, I will make a trip to Sparks. Hopefully, Nan will come too. She thought *it was good to have some sort of direction.* Putting her head in her hands. *I sincerely wish I knew what to do.*

Angelica sat on the bed beating on her drum. She chanted softly with tears in her eyes. Her Drum of Hope gave her peace. *She was glad she had talked to her parents. However, she didn't tell them the whole story. She hadn't been truthful to everybody, even Maggie, she missed Brent. He said he loved her, but then told her she was disposable.*

Her parents wanted her to come home, said they would send money for a bus ticket, but it would be the same old thing and the reason she left.

In her logical mind, Angelica felt she couldn't leave Maggie, as they had to get Brent arrested before he harmed anyone else.

A thought came back to her, *I know we talked about me calling Brent and saying she wanted to see him. He must know by now she is still alive. She knew that would work because he wanted to kill her, or did he? He might be missing her too. She had to end this right away. However, she knew Maggie didn't think it was a good idea.*

Hopping off the bed, she went to find Maggie.

Maggie was in her office. Angelica knocked on the door, "May I come in?"

"Sure, what is happening?" replied Maggie.

Angelica sat down and stared at her hands for a moment, then looked Maggie in the eye, "I would like to call Brent. We believe he knows I am alive, and I could go and meet him."

Maggie interrupted, "No. We talked about this. It is too dangerous! Plus, we talked to Mary about this. She is going to get back to us. She was going to see what the detectives think, so let's be patient."

"Let me finish," said Angelica with a firm look on her face. "We will work through the Sheriff's office, and I will wear a wire or whatever they call it. I know he will want to finish me off or have Fred do it so then we can catch him in the act."

"You have been watching too many cop shows," sighed Maggie. "It sounds good, but it is too dangerous, you're just a child."

"True, but I have learned a lot for my years," snapped Angelica.

Maggie rubbed her chin and said, "good point. But still too dangerous. I couldn't in good faith put you in that position." Maggie put her hands to her face, "let me think about this. Actually, let's sleep on it." Getting up out of her chair, she headed for the office door, "let's go cook dinner."

Angelica gave her a frown, but walked downstairs with her. With Yazoo following.

Chapter Thirteen

Later that evening, Angelica came into the office, "Do you mind if I call home again?"

"Not at all. Getting a little homesick?"

"A little. I guess life wasn't so bad with them, after all. Maybe I am growing up. I miss my mom's voice."

Maggie sniggers under her breath as Angelica skipped off to the bedroom with the phone.

Twenty minutes later, Angelica came back into the office with tears in her eyes. Maggie had forgotten how emotional teenager had gotten. She was all upset with the phone still in her hand."I guess I should go home."

"Wow. What brought this on?" Asked Maggie.

"My Mom had to put my Grandfather in assisted living as he has the start of dementia, and Mom needs help with the younger kids while she spends time at the center with Grandpa."

"Not a problem. I understand. How old is your Grandpa?"

"He is in his late eighties."

"Do you understand what dementia means?"

"No. Not really."

"Dementia means, your Grandpa is beginning to forget the names of your Mom and Dad, maybe even you kids. He has most likely entered the last stages of dementia. That's why he needs full-time care.

At this stage, they are generally unaware of their surroundings, cannot recall recent events, and have confused memories of their past. However, their long term memory is better than their short term; it's sad.

Caregivers and loved ones have to watch for delusional behavior, obsessive behavior as some of the symptoms. Your Grandpa could become anxious, aggressive, agitated, and lose his willpower.

He may begin to wander, have difficulty sleeping, and in some cases, will experience hallucinations. It may be because of these behaviors, is why they placed him in a home," explained Maggie.

"You mean he won't know who I am?' asked Angelica.

"There is a good chance," sighed Maggie.

"I don't know what to do. We need to catch Brent. But I want to see my Grandpa. What should I do?" Whispered Angelica.

"Do what your heart says. Brent will be there, but your Grandpa may not. It might be time to go home. You can always come back. Besides, we girls can catch the bad guys," laughed Maggie.

Angelica looked perplexed, "Maggie, the reason I look the way I do is my Grandpa is

Japanese. He was placed in an internment camp when he was young. His parents were born in Japan. However, he was born in America.

I guess in the 1940's they came and pulled him out of school. He was thirteen or fourteen. The government took everything his family-owned." Angelica paced the office. "I can't imagine a cop coming into school and taking me away to a camp in from of my friends, the embarrassment."

There was a look of anger on her young face, "Then before I was born, after lengthy court battles, he received twenty thousand dollars to repay him for what he lost. That was about one-eighth of the value. His family lost everything, their land, house, family photos, treasures.

But he said, "it gave him a backbone, which he passed on to me," Angelica was crying. "He married a German lady many years later, that he had met in the camp, as she was a teacher assistant. Lily became my Grandma. She died a few years ago from a heart attack."

Maggie was shocked, as she never knew anyone that had been in an internment camp. *She had heard about these camps in college. In 1942, Roosevelt had some 120,000 people of Japanese descent and Japanese American citizens removed from their homes and placed in internment camps.*

The United States justified its actions that those of Japanese ancestry could spy for the Japanese. However, two-thirds of those interned as she remembered, were American citizens, and half of them were children.

Again, if she remembered right, no-one had ever shown disloyalty to the United States. During the entire war, only ten people or so were convicted of spying for Japan, and they were all Caucasian.

The irony of it all. Many of the Japanese Americans in the internment camps were allowed to join the US military.

Angelica went on, "I wonder if the internment had something to do with his memory loss?" Angelica looked perplexed and went on with her story. "Anyway, my Mom married a Spanish Basque, so in our household, we speak Japanese, German, and Spanish, so here I am, Heinze 57." She rubbed her head and, with tears in her eyes, said, "I think I will go home."

"I doubt his internment cause his memory loss. It is probably just old age. However, it's a good choice to go home, though I'll miss you. Pack a bag, and I'll take you to the bus station. I'll call to see when a bus leaves to take you where?" asked Maggie.

Angelica looked at her and quietly said, "Elko."

Before Maggie could call the bus depot, the phone rang, and it was Bud, he sounded terrible, "What is wrong, Bud?" She asked. Angelica's ears perked up.

"I am so sorry. They know you have the girl," he stammered. "They slap me around, and I wouldn't talk, then one of the men grabbed Sadie by the neck and started cutting her, they hurt Sadie to get me to talk," Bud was in tears on the phone.

"Are you two, alright?" Asked Maggie madder than heck. *How could anyone hurt this old man and his dog?*

"We're at the Vet's, "he said, "Sadie lost a lot of blood. If she makes it through the night, the Vet said she should be okay. As far as for me, I will heal. I am so sorry. They don't have your address, just your phone, the description of your car and your license plate."

"How long ago did this happen?" questioned Maggie.

"Maybe twenty-thirty minutes ago."

"Did you report the incident to the Lyon County Sheriff's office?" question Maggie.

"No, I will report it from here at the Vet's office," replied Bud. "I had to get Sadie here right away. Plus, I wanted to make sure you were aware."

"Well, that's good. I am glad you are okay, just take it easy. Do you need anything? When you get home, don't leave the house. Lock all the doors." suggested Maggie.

"No. We will be fine. I am staying here at the Vet's until I know Sadie is okay, then I'll go home. I'll stay in the house. I should have listened to you," sputtered Bud.

"It's okay. I am glad you are okay and prayers for Sadie."

"What happened?" asked Angelica when Maggie hung up.

Maggie told her. "I do think you should go home for your safety. I'll take you to the bus station in Pete's car. I have a blond wig, we'll disguise you, just in case."

"Maggie that won't work, Brent knows I'm from Elko, I told him my whole sad story, because I trusted him. I'm such a dope," cried Angelica.

"Wow, that changes everything. Let me think about this. I assume then they would be watching the bus station." Maggie paces her office. "Do they know where you live in Elko?"

"No. But Brent knows my last name."

"Darn. Darn..."

"Yeah, I screwed up big time."

The phone rang. Maggie didn't recognize the number as it said unavailable, she just let it ring; it went into the answering machine "Hey, Angelica. Dang, you were hard to find. It's time to come home. All is well. No one is mad at you, and we all miss you. If you tell us where you are, we'll come and pick you up, and we'll go for a great dinner. Love and miss you," he said in a soft sexy voice.

Angelica was white with fear, "that was Brent."

Maggie understood, but her mind was working. "Call your parents and warn them. They need to know. He might send his henchmen to go up there looking for you."

A look of panic came across Angelica's face, "I never thought of that," and she quickly dialed her mom.

Maggie couldn't believe how the world had changed in just a few minutes. She called Nan.

Chapter Fourteen

A little over two weeks had gone by since Maggie and Nan had found Angelica. Maggie had grown quite fond of her. However, Maggie also knew she had to go home, but it wasn't safe there now. Pete was still distant, and he again let her know he didn't approve of any of this. If he knew that Brent had their phone number, he would be even more furious.

The next morning Maggie called Bud to check on Sadie. He said, "she's weak, but she made it through the night, so that was good news. She will be staying at the Vets for a few more days before she will be able to come home. I am getting ready to go home now."

"Stay inside and lock your doors." She told him. Maggie didn't believe they would be back, they got what they wanted, but you never know.

Maggie and Nan had planned to go over to Sparks and check out the address in Nan's car. Angelica wanted to come, saying it would be easier for them, as she knew the house. Maggie had to agree. So it was decided they would disguise Angelica, just in case. Brent had called a few more times, with each call he was getting a little more aggressive. But he was smart. He never said his name.

Nan came by in her Subaru Outback with Shep, Yazoo jumped in the back along with Angelica, and they headed for Sparks. Nan used her GPS to take them to 22689 Cottage Parkway, Sparks. It was the upper part of town, with lovely big homes on the hillside.

"That's it, but it looks vacant," stated Angelica

"You're right, and the gate is closed, the curtains were drawn, no cars, papers in the driveway," sighed Maggie. "Angelica, I don't want you to answer his phone calls to find out where he is, so we have a dilemma."

Angelica thought *I'll find out where he is. I'll find him, but I'll not tell Maggie yet what I plan to do. I got Cleo's phone number. This has to end.*

When they got home, there were two messages from Brent, the last one was angry, "Angelica, enough of this, come home. I said I was sorry. I bought you a convertible, a Ford Mustang, and a diamond ring, I want to marry you, please come home now! I'll send the car for you. I am not going to beg anymore. There are plenty of fish in the sea. It is now or never!!" as he hung up.

"Maybe he means it. Maybe he is sorry and truly does love me," cried Angelica.

"Do you, in fact, believe that after what he did to you and what his men did to Bud and Sadie? He told you that you were disposable. Angelia wake up and smell the roses! This is a lie to get you back to hurt or kill you," yelled Maggie.

Angelica held her head in her hands and cried, "You are right, but I love him. He was the first man I ever loved."

"You are a child, he took advantage of you," snapped Maggie. Then she saw the look on Angelica's face and hugged her. She didn't mean to hurt her, even though it was the truth. Maggie thought *I have to get his SOB if it is the last thing I do...*

Unbeknownst to Maggie, Angelica called Cleo to see what was going on and where they had moved, "Hi Cleo, whatsup?'

"Who this?"

"A voice from your past," said Angelica laughing.

"Angelica, is that you?"

"Can't say. But how are you? Can you talk?"

"No. Look for me at the Ace's Ballpark Friday night. That should be a safe place to talk. Bye," whispered Cleo.

Angelica thought *now, how do I tell Maggie?*

Maggie had to set a plan in place. This waiting was driving her crazy. She thought, let's set up a meeting with Brent. She called Nan, who came right over. They all decided to call Mary to see what she could do. She said, "the detective was working on it, but no guarantees. They had a homicide up at Heavenly, and everyone was busy." She continued, " Wait a minute. I will ask him right now as he just came into the office and get back to you."

Within a few minutes, Mary called back, saying, "I talked to Detective Robertson. He didn't like the idea of a civilian wearing a wire, but maybe Angelica could partner up with a young female undercover deputy. It was not out of the ordinary for girls to travel in twos."

"Let's set it up," specified Maggie.

Maggie, Nan, and Angelica were sitting in the home office, discussing what Maggie had in mind when Pete came in. I heard the plan, and I want to be part of it."

They all look at him in shock. Hey, I got used to the kid," he said with a smile, "let's catch this slimeball." They all gave a nervous laugh. Maggie brought him up to speed about Bud. Then Angelica dropped the bomb about Cleo.

Maggie jumped upped, red face, "And when young lady where you going to tell us about this?"

Angelica held her ground, "we have to catch this guy. Brent is smart. I am sure he won't show, he will send Fred. Maybe the undercover officer and I, with the help of Cleo, can do it. Or it could be Cleo is setting me up. But it has to be done. This is our only lead."

"Darn, for a kid, you are smart, and you are right, but don't go off on your own again, please," snapped Maggie.

"I won't," and she embraced both Nan and Maggie.

"Tomorrow night is quilting night. I have a job for the girls. Angelica, you said you were meeting Cleo at the Aces Ball Park on Friday? Angelica shook her head. Sounds good. Let's get this set up," suggested Maggie.

Chapter Fifteen

Wednesday night, they all headed for Fabric Chicks for a quilting lesson. Pete had a 4H meeting, so the house was vacant. Maggie was working on her block and Angelica, her runner, with the cell lying between them, just in case Pete called. About seven o'clock, Maggie's security Ring went off on her phone. There were two men she didn't know at her front door, ringing the doorbell. Angelica, who was sitting next to her, face froze, and she turned white. Everyone saw it. "What is wrong?" asked Maggie.

"That is Fred," whisper Angelica.

"The crud muffin is at my front door. Nan, please call the cops," whispered Maggie.

The Ring videos everything, they tried to open the front door, seeing it was locked. They went around to the back of the house. Unbeknown to them, it also has a Ring. Again, they tried to get into the house to no avail; however, this time, they set off the main security alarm.   After last year's episode, when the house got shot at, Maggie and Pete had placed the house under heavy security.

"Shit, let's get the heck out of here," said one of them. You could hear it all on the Ring.

By the time they ran around to the front of the house, two Douglas County Sheriff's Officers were waiting for them. There just happens to be a sub-station about two blocks from Maggie's house. *Oh my, thought Maggie. But how did they get my address? Crap. It had to come from my Nevada plates.*

Maggie called the Douglas County Sheriff's office and told them she had it all on video and was pretty sure; these were the same two men who beat up an older man and cut on his dog in Dayton, in Lyon County. Bud Freer has filed a report on the incident.

Also, she suspected they were involved in the sex trafficking of young girls. Is it possible to lock them up with no bail? Hopefully, the cop shop could keep them for twenty-four to forty-eight hours.

"Well, at least for now, we got rid of two of the henchmen," stated Maggie. "Here is what I want to happen at the Ball Park on Friday if you guys are willing," and she laid out the plan.

Ginger Knowles was a cute little blond officer. She looked to be about eighteen, although she was twenty-six. Both Angelica and Ginger wore wires. There were four plainclothes Reno police officers spread around the outside of the ballpark, plus Maggie and Nan.

Betty was working at the main ballpark gate as a customer service person. She sometimes worked there part-time. Tonight, Betty could observe the front of the park. Pete was in the parking garage so he could watch the main gate area also.

Beth and her husband, Jeff, a retired police officer, were inside at the ball game, he was watching a wireless camera from the front gate area. *So the bases were covered*, thought Maggie laughing to herself.

Around ten, Ginger and Angelica were flirting with one of the officers, mainly to look like they were going to solicit a trick. As Angelica started to walk off with him, she spotted Cleo.

Angelica whispered to the officer, "there's Cleo." Leaving him, she walked over to Cleo.

"Hi" Angelicia couldn't believe her eyes, Cleo looked terrible, she had aged, Cleo must have lost ten pounds. She hugged Cleo and could feel her bones. "How have you been?"

"Horrible, I want out, but can't, he watches my every move. He is watching us right now. Nothing makes him happy. You are in danger. He wants you dead," whispered Cleo.

"I can get you out," stated Angelica

"Only one way out, that's death," sighed Cleo.

"Not true, look at me, I am out."

"I gotta go, they are coming, watch out, they will grab you. Brent will kill you this time." And she walked off.

Angelica looked up to see two guys coming toward her, and she didn't recognize either of them. The four officers plus Ginger, Maggie, and Nan watch it all too, as they were also closing in on the men. Nan was the closest to Angelica when she saw one of the guys pull out a gun. She tackled Angelica, taking her to the ground with a thud. Maggie quickly took out her Taser and used it on him. He went down squirming, and one of the officers grabs the weapon from the ground.

The other officers tackled the second guy, and they cuffed them both. Betty, Beth, and Jeff observed the whole event. Most of the people didn't even know what happened. The game had ended, and everyone was watching the fireworks. Angelica looked for Cleo, but she was gone.

Well, this didn't turn out as planned. They didn't find out where Brent was living, thought

Maggie. *We didn't find out anything new, back to the drawing board.*

Brent observed the whole event in front of the Ball Park from the first floor of the parking building. He was not happy. *Was Cleo in on this? Did she know it was a trap? He would find out one way or another, and she would be sorry. He hated losing another gal from his stable as that was lost revenue. He had already lost Angelica and that one he would take care of personally the next time.*

Brent, now in his late thirties, was a pro at the business, he had been doing it for ten years, and he owned some influential people. Currently, about twenty girls and two guys worked for him. He had five more young girls coming in from Central

America that the cartel had kidnapped. They ranged from twelve to eighteen.

Brent knew the more influential the customer, the younger they liked the girl. But, Brent wanted the girl to be at least sixteen. So he would sell the younger ones to another dealer. *You have to have some ethics,* and he laughed to himself.

He hopped in his Mercedes and drove out of the parking garage to find Cleo. She should be at the local bar. They needed to talk.

Pete observed the man watching what was going on down on the field. He looked angry. Pete crept up as close as he dared to get a description of the man. Maybe nothing, but you never know. He watched the man get into his Mercedes and drive off. Pete wrote down the license plate and noted the car was black and relatively new. He would pass it on.

Brent and Pete weren't the only people observing the goings-on at the Park. A tall man stood in the shadows on the second floor of the parking garage, smoking one cigarette after another. He was hired to find Cleo and bring her home. He saw her walk off toward the river and go under the bridge. He thought, *A lot of homeless live down there, maybe that is where she is living?*

Gray-haired Alan Trent had been a Private Investigator ever since he retired from the Phoenix Police Dept over fifteen years ago. He was creeping up on sixty-five and thinking of retiring, solving missing person's cases, or gathering material for a divorce, was getting old.

A couple of weeks ago, Cleo Thompson's dad came to his office and hired him to find his only daughter, as her mother is dying from pancreatic cancer. He said Cleo had met a guy online last year, supposedly fell in love, and went to meet him in Nevada. Since she was eighteen, there was no way they could stop her. She's an adult. They heard from her every couple of weeks. But haven't heard a word from her in over three months and with her mom ill and all. Alan took the case, plus Nevada is cooler than Arizona in the summer.

He thought *it was easy to track Cleo to Reno, plus she had been busted for soliciting in Douglas County a few weeks back. Her address from her Dad was cold, but nosing around, he found where she hung out. Tonight was interesting though, all the cops involved. He was going to check with a friend at the police station to see what was going on.*

Putting out another cigarette, he got into his old white Toyota and drove to the first floor to park. He would walk from there to the river.

Chapter Sixteen

Cleo walked down the path under the bridge to a big rock. It was a beautiful June night. Sitting on a rock, she watched the river, which was high and moving fast from Lake Tahoe's snow runoff.

She sat there, smoking a cigarette as she was coming down from the drugs she had taken. Cleo was also drinking from a pint bottle of vodka in a brown paper bag to help her even out.

Angelica looked so good, and she got away. I'll never get away. How could I've been so stupid to think Fred loved me. He worked for Brent. It was their plan all along to have me hooking. I can't go home. I'm too ashamed. Cleo dipped her hand in the fast-moving water. It was cold. *I wonder what it would be like if I slipped into the water and floated downstream, would I drown?* She sat there, finishing her cigarette and drinking the last of the vodka in a brown paper bag, contemplating what to do.

In anger, she threw the empty vodka bottle with the bag into the bushes with a thud. Without thinking, she quietly, slipped into the water, soon as the water hit her back, "Damn, this is cold," The cold water sort of sober her up, but it was too late. She tried to get out, even though she was in the calm part of the river, the water was moving too fast. She thought, *what the hell, let's end it here.*

Putting her face in the water, she floated in the fast-moving water, just bearing the cold. Her lungs started to burn, wanting air. She refused to take her face out of the water. Finally, after a few minutes or so, she raises her face to breathe as she thought her lungs would explode.

By now, she was in the rapids of the river. She tries putting her head up to breathe through her mouth. When she started coughing and sputtering, swallowing lots of water, plus her clothes were weighing her down. She was so numb with cold; she couldn't even lift her arms to swim or scream for help. Cleo's body was bouncing on the rocks, but she was so cold she didn't feel any pain.

Finally, she gave up, and the water enveloped her. Her body floated into a calm part of the river, and the current washed her over to some willow bushes. Her clothes got tangled up in the bushes, and she stayed. Nineteen-year-old Cleo was free and at peace at last.

Alan walked down under the bridge, looking for Cleo. It was dark, so he pulled out his flashlight to see the path. He saw a couple of homeless people, a man, and a woman with their dog around their campfire.

"Hi folks, Have you seen a tall blond girl go by in the last half hour?"

"Why? You a cop," replied the man with missing teeth.

"Nope, I'm her Dad," lied Alan.

"Sorry, you look like a cop. Nope, no one has gone by." claimed the woman, who needed a bath and her hair combed.

"Thanks. Have a nice evening. Sorry to have bothered you all," stated Alan with a smile.

"No problem, buddy. I hope you find your daughter."

Alan gave him a salute and went walking up the path. He walked for a quarter of a mile of so toward Reno, past several homeless camps, but no one was home or they were in bed. *Maybe she walked up the bank and left the River. Perhaps she is working,* he thought.

Deciding to head back, he shined his flashlight on the river to see if there was a bridge to cross over the river on. The Truckee River was high, and the water was moving too fast for even a man-made bridge, so that was out. Frustrated, he headed back to his car. Dead-end here. Guess I'll go to the Police station to see what all the action was about earlier at the ballpark.

Alan stopped by the Reno Police Station. He knew Sargeant Mike Nichols worked there. However, he was not on shift, and wouldn't be at work until tomorrow. Damn, I am hitting a blank wall. Think I will get a beer and something to eat. Tomorrow is another day.

When Maggie, Nan, and Angelica arrived home, they were concerned, as Brent hadn't called. He had been calling two to three times a day, but he hadn't called today. Angelica tried calling Cleo, but it went into her answering system.

"I hope she is all right, she was so thin. I could tell she was on drugs," stated Angelica.

"She didn't know it was a trap on our side. However, she may have known about Brent's henchman," chimed Nan.

What is frustrating is we know nothing new," sighed Maggie. "I am not sure where to go from here."

Pete came in about this time, he had been listening, "Maybe we could ask Mary if she can find out who got the information about our address and who received the information. Plus, I have a description of a man who was watching the whole event, his car and license plate," He had a big smile on his face. "It may be nothing, but let's see."

"Wow. That is great. I'm so proud of you for helping." They all shook their heads in agreement.

Peter described the man saying, "he was in his late thirties, medium build, blond hair and walked with a little limp."

Angelica jumped up with fear on her face and said, "That's Brent. So he was there. I wonder what he planned to do with me?"

Even though it was after eleven at night, Maggie picked up the phone and promptly called Mary. "We have a plate NV 646SAO for you to run as soon as possible, this may be the bad guy. Also, can you find out how someone can get my plate info if they are not in law enforcement?"

Mary s groggily answered, "I'm not sure I can find out how they got your home address, but I will try. Running the plate will be easy. I will call you in the morning.

"Thank you, and I am sorry to be calling so late, but this is extremely important. Tonight didn't go as planned. Will fill you in tomorrow," shared Maggie.

"Let's get something to eat. I can't think when I'm so hungry, and I need a cigarette," sighed Nan.

Maggie made a face at her as they all hopped in the jeep and headed to Denny's for food.

Chapter Seventeen

The next day, Brent was pacing in his office; things were falling apart. He couldn't find Cleo last night, four of his men were now in jail. *What the shit is going on? The cops were playing hardball, according to his attorney, he can't bail his men out.*

Frustrated, he called his attorney Ray Fromberg again, "Hey Ray, you need to get Fred, Alex, Jose, and Craig out of jail on bail quickly."

Ray said, "as I said, no can do. I already checked into this. Fred and Alex beat up a senior and cut up his dog in Lyon County. That's a crime against a senior, that's a severe situation. Then they tried to break into a house in Douglas County. Fred and Alex have been busy breaking laws.

Brent thought *if you only knew how many laws they had broke...*

They'll all have to go to court to have the bail set. Jose is an illegal, Craig, an ex-felon who had a gun. Nothing is looking good. All four will be in jail for at least forty-eight hours or more."

"Fred and Alex have already been in jail for over forty-eight hours. I don't want to hear that you can't get them out, do what you can quickly," sneered Brent. "I pay you enough, plus I have pictures that you don't want to surface."

It was quiet on the other end, "I will do what I can," snapped the attorney. *I hate this guy thought Ray.*

"You better and fast, I need Fred," as Brent hung up.

And where in the hell is Cleo? She didn't come home last night, so she owes me money. Just wish Fred had dumped Angelica down a mine shaft instead of in Sutro Tunnel. Stupid idiot! If he had done what I told him to do, none of this would be happening.

Brent didn't like it when things were not under his control. *Maybe I'll give the girls a rest until this all blows over... damn that's a lot of money to lose. Angelica will pay dearly for all this trouble.*

It was a cool morning for late June, as the toothless man crawled out of his tent to take a pee. He walked down by the river bank, as he was writing his name in the river, he notices something in the water down about fifty feet from him. It looked like clothes caught in the bushes. *Shoot, this may be my lucky day, new clothes for Mama.* Shaking his willy, and zipping his pants up, he walked down to the bushes.

As he climbed down to the willows, he noticed it's a blonde woman wearing those clothes. He thought, *darn, this may be the girl that the man was looking for last night. Having a body here will bring the cops. Can't have that.* Picking up a branch, he loosens the body from the bushes to let it float further downstream. He thought *it would have been great to have the clothes, but I don't need any cops busting us* as he headed back to his tent.

Cleo's body floated for a couple of hundred yards when she hit the rapids again, and away it went.

The next morning, Maggie had the board out and was reviewing the information to it. *I am missing something, yeah more information. We need to meet with Cleo again. Darn, I got to think about all of this.*

Chapter Eighteen

Mary called the first thing that morning, "The car belongs to a Brent Stevens, it is a 2018 Mercedes, and he lives at 22689 Cottage Parkway, Sparks. I also found who requested to run your plate, it wasn't easy, but computers are fabulous.

It was a lawyer by the name of Ray Fromberg. It seems he works for Stevens." Mary stopped for a moment, flipping some papers. "He was the guy who bailed out the two girls we arrested a while back."

Mary paused, "Now I have some bad news. This morning, they found the body of a young girl in the Truckee River. It sounds like the girl Angelica met last night. I'll let you know when I have more details."

"Wow, Mary, you have been busy. The address doesn't help as he has moved. But the lead on his attorney helps. Let us know what you find out about the body, and I pray it is not Cleo. Thank you so much," whispered Maggie.

Maggie called Nan and gave her the information. Then she almost skipped out of her office, yelling to Pete and Angelica to meet in the kitchen. They all needed to talk about this and what they can do. By the time they all were seated in the kitchen, Nan arrived.

Sitting around the kitchen table drinking coffee, she told them what Mary had said about Brent and the body.

Angelica asked, "May I use the cell to try and call Cleo?"

Maggie slid it over to her, and Angelica dialed Cleo's number. No answer as it went into her voice mail. There was a look of fear on her face and tears in her eyes. "He must have killed her because she was talking to me."

"That's not true. First, we are not sure the body is Cleo, and if it is, we don't know how she died. So don't go blaming yourself," snapped Nan.

"Good point," agreed Maggie. "Now, let's figure what we do next."

She went to her chalkboard that she had left in the kitchen and started in:

1 We know his name. Brent Stevens

2 We know where he lived. 22689 Cottage Parkway, Sparks.

3. We have the plate of the truck, which dumped Angelica.

4. We know the owner of the red Ford pickup truck, Fred Jones. He lived at the same address as Brent

5. We know or think we know the first names of two of the girls, Tanya and Cleo.

6. We have pictures of Angelica with her bruises, and of course, the gag used.

7. We have Brent license Plates 646SAO and his address, which is no good. But we know he drives a black Mercedes.

8. We have his lawyer's name, Ray Fromberg.

Maggie stopped and then quickly ran upstairs to her office and grabbed a phone book, she when through the pages looking up Fromberg's name, and sure enough, he works in Reno. She came back down the stairs to share in information.

"Ray Fromberg is a criminal attorney. His address is 20945 Arlington, Reno. The phone is 775-555-9260. Shall we give him a call, " asked Maggie. " The other thing we can do is find out who owns the property where Brent lived. They may have a forwarding address."

Everyone just sat there not sure, Pete finally said, "Should we contact the police?"

"I am not sure we have enough to bring them in. I'll call Mary and see what Detective Robertson thinks," stated Maggie.

Everyone agreed to that.

Chapter Nineteen

After eating a big breakfast at the Sands, Alan headed for the Reno Police Station. He loved the smell when he walked into the station. Walking up the desk sergeant, whose name tag said, Jones. "Hi. Alan Trent," as he flashes his PI and retired Phoenix police badge. " I like to see Sergeant Mike Nichols if it's possible."

"Let me check to see if he is in," Jones went to the phone and made a call. Jones laughed. I will send him down."

Coming back to the counter, Jones pointed down the hall, "He is in. Straight down, second door on the right."

"Thanks." Alan gave him a salute and headed down the hall. Approaching the second door on the right, he knocked.

"Come in, you tall drink of water," said the voice on the other side. Alan went on in and shook Mike's hand as he got up to welcome Alan. "What are you doing in Nevada?"

"Looking for a nineteen-year-old girl named Cleo Thompsen. Think she might have gotten herself wrapped up in prostitution. Have you guys busted her?"

"Let me look," and punched keys on his computer. "Nope, but I see, she was busted in Douglas County."

"Yeah, I knew about that. Last night I followed her to the Ball Park, she was talking to a couple of other girls, then left and headed for the river, right before all heck broke loose at the ballpark. By the way, what was that all about?"

"We had an undercover gal with a young girl who was being forced into sex trafficking. Trying to catch the boss, but just got minnows."

"Cleo knew the girl as they hugged and talked for a few minutes, and as I said, Cleo headed for the river. I did go down looking for her, but she must have walked up a bank," explained Alan.

"Is this Cleo a tall blonde on the skinny side?" Asked Mike.

"Yeah, a little too skinny, might be on drugs, stated Alan.

"Well, we may have found her for you. We fished a body out of the river this morning. It sounds like it fits your girl," sighed Mike.

"Where is the body now, so I can verify it's her? Alan asked.

"At the morgue under Jane Doe." Mike wrote down the address and handed it to Alan. "Hope it's not her."

"Yeah, me too. Other than this, how have you been? How is Connie? Do you like working here better than Phoenix?" asked Alan.

The two friends talked for a few minutes catching up on old times. "If you are here for a while, come on over tonight and have dinner,' invited Mike. He wrote down his home address and phone, handing it to Alan.

"It all depends on what I find at the morgue. I will call if I can make it." With that, Alan stood up and again shook Mike's hand. "Thanks for the info."

They shoulder bumped, and Alan headed for the Morgue.

Damn, Alan hated going to the morgue. He didn't like the smell or the glare. Going inside, he asked the woman at the desk, flashing his badges if he could see the girl from the river.

"Are you related?"

"No. Not sure if she might be my client's daughter," respond Alan.

"Just fill out this paperwork to allow you to go back," as she handed him a single page.

Alan took about three minutes to fill and handed it back to her. She walked away and called someone. "Take a seat. Someone will be here shortly to take you down."

"Thanks." But she was already on her computer.

Alan took a seat and glanced at the magazines on the table, his lucky day, Sport's Illustrated Swim Edition. He was halfway through when a middle-aged man with gray temples wearing a white coat came over to him, "Hello, I am Dr. Jameston, the Coroner on duty. Please follow me."

They walked down a hall into a big bright room with all kinds of chambers. Dr. Jameston walked over to one and pushed the button. The gurney came out with a body under a sheet. The Dr. pulled the sheet back.

Alan took a good look, same clothes Cleo was wearing last night stacked beside her, it looked like her."May I touch? She has a tattoo of a butterfly on her chest, according to her Dad."

The Dr. pulled the sheet back to show her chest, and there it was... the butterfly tattoo. This was Cleo. "How did she die?"

"I don't believe it was a homicide. It looks like she drowned as her lungs were full of water. We did find meth and alcohol in her system. Possibly she was drinking to come down from the drugs. So she could have stumbled and fallen into the river. With the water high, cold, and moving fast this time of year, she probably couldn't get out."

Alan shook his head. This was the part of his job he hated to tell the parents that their only daughter is dead. "Thank you, Dr. Her name is Cleo Thompson, 19 from Phoenix, Ariz. I will notify her parents."

Alan walked out with a heavy sigh. Darn, you never get used to this. When he got outside, he called Mr. Thompson to give them the sad news and close the case. Tonight he would get drunk with Mike and maybe tomorrow he would head for home. However, he sort of liked the area; perhaps I will stay awhile.

Chapter Twenty

Ray called Brent, "You are not going to like what I have to say, the police fished a body out of the river, and it was Cleo."

"Damn, You are right, not something I wanted to hear. Well, that explains why I couldn't reach her," replied Brent. *He was not happy. What in the heck is going on? How did she end up in the river?*

"The boys won't be going to court until next week, probably around Thursday," Ray continued to say. "Not sure what they will do with Fred, he committed that crime against a senior, and that doesn't look good. They are holding him in Yerington in the Lyon County Jail, which looks down on Senior crimes. Plus, Douglas wants him next for an attempted break-in. So he will be seeing some jail time."

"Damn, Damn, Well, do what you can. I need Fred pronto," whined Brent. *That little snot Angelica has cost me a lot, now to get even.*

Brent went storming out of his office to find Miguel. He had a job for him.

Maggie was concerned that they hadn't heard from Brent since this all went down. He also knew where she lived and that Angelica was there. They were all sitting in Detective Robertson's office, and Maggie voiced her concerns.

"We can put Angelica in a safe place until this all blows over."

Maggie, Nan, Pete, and Angelica all looked at each other. Pete stated, "no offense officer, but we will keep Angelica close. We know that Brent will try something, but hopefully, we'll be prepared. Can you put pressure on his attorney? Or should we call him?"

"I can't pressure the attorney. Maybe you should call him. It might scare out something. I can give you an officer to stay with you to protect

Angelica.   Personally, I believe he will send someone to capture her so that he can do her in. So you all could be in danger as long as she at your home," warned the detective.

Pete looked at Maggie, "What's new? This isn't our first rodeo," and they all laughed.

Angelica asked in a whisper, "Did you guys find Cleo?"

Robertson shuffles through some papers, "Yes, we did, she washed up this morning from the river and was identified by a PI who works for her parents. It's not a homicide. She could have fallen or slipped in."

"Or was pushed. Though I believe Cleo committed suicide. She said the only way out was to die," whisper Angelica with tears.

"Crap," said Nan, "which means Brent really will try something. He probably blames Angelica for her death. Loss of revenue!" Nan had an angry look on her face.

"We will take an officer to protect Angelica," chimed Pete.

"This is all well and good, but we need a plan. I will call Fromberg and see what thorn I can put under his saddle," sneered Maggie.

They discussed how to keep Fred in jail. What Robertson wanted was to flush out Brent, so they needed to put a plan in place. They all decided to think about it and come up with something quickly.

Chapter Twenty-One

Maggie called Fromberg's office and set up a meeting. He would think it was a criminal matter. She had an appointment for two o'clock tomorrow.

They moved Angelica to the basement of the house. No one could get in there from outside. They would have to come through the house. The female officer was her roommate.

If Angelica went outside, they would disguise her as an older woman. Maggie, Nan, and Pete tried to think of everything.

Maggie told Angelica, "Yazoo will take care of you. He will sense your fear. Just tell him 'to fetch,' and he will go after the bad guy." Maggie hoped they were ready for whatever trouble was coming.

On Thursday, Maggie, Pete, and Angelicia went to see Fromberg. They were escorted into his office by his secretary.

"Hi, I am Maggie McDonald, my husband Pete, and my niece Angelica." Maggie watched his face change when she said Angelica's name. "My niece has got herself into some trouble, and we need an attorney to help us," Maggie had a story prepared to tell him.

"What kind of legal trouble?" asked Fromberg.

"It has to do with Sex Trafficking. She was being forced into prostitution. She wants to have the boss man arrested, but we don't know how to go about it." stated Maggie, "we don't want the publicity, you know to save the girl from any embarrassment..."

Fromberg's face lost color, " This sounds like a police matter. Have you contacted the police?

"No, not yet, as I said, we were hoping to keep it quiet for Angelica's sake, " stated Pete.

"And who would this person be, and do you have any proof. Sex trafficking is a serious accusation," questioned Fromberg."

"We have proof. His name is Brent Stevens," stated Pete.

Fromberg started waving his hands, "I cannot take your case, as Stevens is a client of mine. I do not believe he is guilty of this type of crime. He is a reputable businessman dealing in real estate."

"Reputable my butt, he rapes children. This is one of them..." sneered Maggie.

"I am going to have to ask you to leave," growled Fromberg.

"We are, and I wouldn't want you as an attorney if you defend people like Stevens," claimed Pete as they walked out the door.

When they got to the car, they all laughed. "Think we put a thorn under their saddle. Now we see what happens. At least Fromberg was honest and said that he represents Stevens. We best tell Detective Robertson," smiled Maggie.

Chapter Twenty-Two

Fromberg couldn't get to the phone fast enough after they left, "You won't believe who was in my office seeking criminal help? Angelica."

"Do you still have her there?" asked Brent.

"No. I kicked her and her Aunt and Uncle out of my office, I said I represent you, and you're an honest businessman."

"Damn, you stupid fool, they're working with the cops, and they must have known you are my attorney. Thanks for defending me... damn damn. I have to get that girl," as he hung up. Brent thought *she is costing me a fortune... good thing I have a few cops, judges, and politicians in my database. Time to call them in.*

Maggie called Nan to tell her what happened at Fromberg office. Soon as she heard Nan's voice, she knew something was wrong. "Okay, what is going on?"

Nan replied in a whisper, The shots didn't work for Bill, and he has to start radiation every day for eight weeks."

"Doggonit! I was praying it would work."

"So were we. But things will get better," sighed Nan. "We just wanted the shots to work. The other bad news I won't be able to help you much with this Brent guy."

"Not too worried, that is the least of your problems, we will work this out. There is still the quilting club," stated Maggie. Maggie was devastated not to have Nan's help, but Bill needed her more. They talked some more about Bill before they hung up.

Maggie sat in her chair, with her hands on her head, *I know all will be okay, but darn, why Bill?*

Chapter Twenty-Three

Maggie thought I've got to do some more research on sex trafficking. Maybe it will help me understand all of this a little more. Like how do these guys get away with it? She thought of Epstein. He got away with it for years. Of course, he owned some powerful people, does Brent?

She opened her computer and google sex trafficking...holy moly! There was a porn site from Canada that had over 42 billion hits with thousands of videos of children being raped. Maggie cried, *how can this be?* More information stated 2017 Internation stats, there were over four million sex slaves, 79% adults, and 21% children – 99% were women and girls. She also read that U.S. Immigration and Customs Enforcement have arrested over 5000 traffickers so far, and yet it still goes on.

Maggie rubbed her head angrily and thought, *I will never to able to stop all this crime, but I hopefully can get Brent Stevens off the streets and save a few girls.*

The Ring went off on her phone, she looked, and there was a mail carrier at the door. "He stated, I need a signature for this package." *Funny, I have nothing coming, maybe Pete.*

She hollered to Pete in the bedroom, "There is a package for you at the front door."

Pete responded, coming into her office, "I don't have something coming," as he viewed the Ring.

They both went downstairs to the door. Maggie stood back in the kitchen as Pete opened the front door, talking through the storm door, "Yes. May I help you."

"I have a package for Maggie McDonald that needs a signature," said the voice with an accent.

Pete looked at Maggie, shook her head no. Pete opened the storm door to sign when he noticed the carrier had a gun pointed at him. Pete backs up inside the house, as the carrier came into the hallway."Where is Angelica?" The carrier demanded.

Pete quickly backed away from the guy, as Maggie came around through the kitchen doorway and tasered the guy. Down he went, with Pete grabbing the gun. Maggie promptly yelled for the officer downstairs. In no time, they cuffed the carrier, and a patrol car came.

In searching him, the ID stated he's Miguel Sanchez, who had several wants, plus today's attempted break-in and assault, he was promptly charged as they read him his rights, but Miguel said nothing except he wanted his attorney, "Fromberg." Maggie and Pete didn't believe in coincidence. They knew Brent had sent him.

After everything calmed down, Maggie hugged her husband, and said, "this Taser was the best birthday gift you could have given me." And they both laughed.

Maggie, Angelicia, and Pete talk to Detective Robinson, especially how brazen Brent was to send a henchman to their home. It was decided to do another sting operation with the Douglas County Sheriff's Office and the Reno Police involved. Angelica would call Brent and set up a meeting. They suspected he would know the cops would be there too, so they'll have to be real cagey.

They planned for Angelica to meet Brent in broad daylight in a busy Reno restaurant. She would be wearing a wire, plus be with a female officer, and there would be many undercover cops in the restaurant.

Maggie thought it all sounded good, but she was leery of putting Angelica in such a dangerous spot. *What if he shot her? Or had one of his minions kill her? No, he will want to do it himself. However, I have a little insurance plan.*

The police wired Maggie's phone so that everyone could listen in on the call. That evening, Angelica called Brent. It rang a few times before he picked up. "Hi, it is about time you called me back."

"Sorry, but I didn't know what to say," whispered Angelica.

"Say you want to come home. I have missed you so much," Brent said in a sexy voice.

Angelica looked at Maggie and thought, *what if he is missing me.* Maggie saw that look and shook her head.

"I would like to meet with you before I come home. No offense, but you left me for dead. How do I know you won't do it again?" Questioned Angelica.

"I am so sorry for what happened. I can promise it won't happen again. Fred should have been kinder to you," said Brent, who was being very careful about what he said. He suspected the phone is bugged, as he knows she is working with the cops.

Angelica didn't know what to say at first. "Fred had nothing to do with it. You took the belt to me."

"Angelica baby, you are exaggerating, you were drunk and fell getting out of the pool," replied Brent.

Now Angelica was mad, but she had to carry this through, "Let's meet at the Sands Hotel/Casino in Reno, Mel's Diner at four tomorrow, and we can further discuss this matter."

Brent figured this was a trap, but two can play, "Sounds good, I look forward to seeing you." Saying, "I love you," as he hung up.

Angelica hung up the phone," I wasn't drunk, and I didn't fall."

"We know that," said Maggie, "I have the pictures of your bruises."

Maggie gave Angelica a big hug, "You did good, that was hard. Now we lay the rest of the groundwork."

Chapter Twenty-Four

Brent though after he hung up, Two can play this game. I will have several of my men in the restaurant, and I think a call to one of my cop friends is needed at this time.

Wednesday night was quilting night. So when Nan, Angelicia, and Maggie showed up, there was lots of talk about what was happening tomorrow.

The group decided that Betty and Beth's husband, Jeff would be there together eating in the restaurant. Beth couldn't get away due to the quilting store. Pete and Maggie were going to be there, as they both have Certified Concealed Weapon permits. Nan couldn't make it as she was taking Bill for treatment. Maggie felt between the quilting club and the cops they had it covered. So let the fun begin.

The next day Maggie drove Angelica and a redheaded cop named Robin MacPherson over to the Sands. Everyone else was already there. As Maggie was walking in, she felt nervous. She had this funny feeling stuck in the pit of her stomach. Whenever that occurs, something goes wrong. Looking around, all looked good, and she saw Betty and Jeff in one booth. Pete was at the counter.

The three of them were seated at a booth to wait for Brent. Angelica was on the inside with Robin sitting on the outside. Maggie sat across from them in the booth. It was only three forty-five.

The waitress came over and took their order. They just ordered drinks. The three of them were like nervous wrecks. Well, the cop wasn't worried.

Angelica said, "I am so nervous I have to pee." Maggie and Robin looked at her, and Robin said, "I will go with you, just in case." And they both got up to leave the booth.

Maggie watched them walk toward the casino to the bathrooms. The minutes flew by. It was now after four and no Brent. Actually, where is Angelica, *what is taking her so long? A good ten minutes had passed.*

Angelica came out of the bathroom stall to Robin holding a gun on her. "What??? Why? Stammered Angelica looking at the gun. Robin had the faucets running to drown out any sounds.

Angelica was frozen in fear. Quickly, Robin removed Angelica's wire without saying anything and dumped it in the garbage. "Because the boss man said he wanted to see you," stated Robin. "Now, let's go."

Maggie got nervous and went to the bathroom to check on the girls, no one there. "Crap" as she ran out to the restaurant and told everyone, "They're gone. Didn't anyone hear anything?" she snarled. Everyone shook their head no.

Half the restaurant got up to leave, meeting outside. The main question was, where did they go, and did Brent have them. Angelica's wire was no longer working, so it must have been removed. Maggie went to her Jeep and checked her GPS. It was working and tracking Angelica.

"Hey, you guy, I got her on my GPS," she shouted, the officers and Pete came running over. "I planted a personal GPS device in her boot, for just in case," she said with a smile.

Chapter Twenty-Five

Alan Trent hadn't gone back to Arizona yet. He didn't have any family or pets, so there was no rush to get back to the heat. He had spent a couple of days staying at the Sands Casino. Today, as he was getting ready to leave, he spotted two girls, going across the Casino floor. Alan recognized one of the girls as the girl that had met Cleo at the Ball Park. And it looked like she was being escorted out of the Casino. She had a look of fear on her face, and the girl behind her seemed to be holding something, maybe a weapon on her as they walked out.

Alan decided to follow. They went out of the door first. He followed. His car was parked closer to where they were going. He watched to see them climb into a black Mercedes. Writing down the license plate, NV 646SAO, he pulled out in front of them.

He watches the Mercedes, which was about four cars back. It was headed down Virginia St.

when it got to Center, it made a turn. Alan crossed through a business parking lot and came out on Center, this time behind the Mercedes. Alan was thankful his car looked like everyone else, an older white Toyota.

This may be a waste of time, but what the heck I have plenty of time, he thought as he followed the car.

Before they left the Sands, One of the officers got a call from Detective Robinson. He informed them that her husband found officer Robin MacPherson tied and gagged in her home.

Maggie thought, *then who is the officer with Angelica?* Batting herself on the head, *you stupid idiot, she was a plant. Brent has Angelica. But how did he know what was coming down? He must have a cop or a secretary on the payroll in one of the Departments.*

Pete jumped in the Jeep with Maggie and Yazoo, and they started following the GPS, with the officers following them. The car was going up Center then over to Wells and then headed up Moana to Skyline then to S. McCarren. Then it turned up on Mayberry Drive. He was going in different directions as a precaution, or did he know he was being followed?

"Looks like he wants to make sure he is not being followed," stated Pete.

"Yeah, but it looks like he is finally stopping. Hurry!" informed Maggie.

Alan noticed that the car was going in all different directions. Maybe the driver had made him. On McCarran, Alan pulled over and called Mike his friend at the Reno Police Department.

Talking to a Desk Sgt, they finally put his call through to Sgt. Nichols.

"Hey Mike, This is Alan, and yes, I am still in town. I may be on a wild goose chase, but the girl I saw talking to Cleo was escorted out of the Sands by a red hair girl who was holding some sort of weapon on her. I have been following and have the license plate of 2018 black Mercedes 646SAO. Can you run it ASAP?"

"Will do, but I need to let you know you are in the middle of a sting operation and that girl is in trouble, they want her dead. The car currently has been located on 223567 Mayberry, an apartment complex," informed Mike. "The car belongs to a Brent Stevens, no wants on him," stated Mike.

"Wow, that was fast," laughed Alan. "Thanks for your help.

Alan turned on his GPS and headed for 223567 Mayberry.

Angelica couldn't believe what had happened. She was sitting next to Brent, and he was angry. Robin sitting on the other side of Angelica, tore off the wig, and what the heck. *It was a guy in the officer's garb!*

"Good job Nick, I will pay you well for this job, as this lady has cost me a lot of money," sneered Brent.

The Mercedes driver said, "I am sure that we aren't being followed, but to be safe, I am going in all different directions. It looks good now so that we can go to the Condo."

"I am looking forward to some fun with you, Angelica, before I end it for once and all," again sneered Brent as he affectionately rubs her face, then slapped her hard. "Nick. Gag and tie her up."

Taking a scarf from around his neck, Nick slapped her hard to get her gagged and placed zip ties on her hands.

Maggie, Pete, and the officers arrived at Mayberry, seeing it was a Condo complex, where did the Mercedes go.

Pete and Maggie had got their first. Pete hollered to the cops, "There's the black Mercedes. I saw the same one at the ballpark. It's parked in front of C287. The Condo on the end."

Pete and Maggie stayed in the Jeep. This was a police matter. The officers crept up to the front door, with guns drawn. "This is the Reno Police, come out with your hands up," as they shouted through the door. No reply.

Again the officers called out and still no reply. Finally, one officer took an ax from his patrol car to the door while standing off to the side. The door broke easily and in they went. They came out within minutes, saying, "all clear. No one is in there."

Maggie and Yazoo went running up to see what was going on. Pete followed. Once inside, they saw that there had been a struggle. Angelica's boots were on the floor. Maggie thought, *so there went the GPS. The back window was broken, so that's how they must have gotten out. But where is Angelica?* Maggie ran over to see if Angelica was laying down there hurt as it was a six-foot drop or if she was gone. Maggie didn't see her.

Yazoo started barking at the closet door, the police opened it quickly, with guns drawn, inside was a man dressed in police officer clothes with his hands up. "Don't shoot. Don't shoot." The officers cuffed him and led him outside to a patrol car. The officer placed him in the back seat and came back into the condo.

Maggie exclaimed, "That is the cop who was with Angelica. At least those are the clothes Robin had on, oh my gosh, it was a man!"

Yazoo went running outside and around the building. He was barking all the way. Everybody followed. They're trying to hide in the shrubs, was a skinny man in a chauffeur's uniform. He looked hurt from the fall, or at least he was hugging his knee.

However, Yazoo was barking at another bush, but wagging his tail at the same time. Maggie couldn't believe her eyes. There in the bushes was Angelica, gagged and beaten, it looked like she had passed out.

Maggie ran over to her and picked up her head, removing the gag, part of her clothes had been ripped off, and she was severely beaten. Yazoo started licking her. Maggie was holding her as Angelica began coming around. Angelica eyes open, and she looked up and saw Maggie. Grabbing Maggie every so tightly, the tears started flowing, "he was going to rape and kill me."

"Do you know where he went?" Asked one of the officers.

"No. As soon as he saw my GPS device, he slapped me around, then threw me out the window. I crawl under a bush for safety and must have passed out. I didn't see him get out of the apartment."

"Are you okay? Do you feel like anything broken? Sprained?" Asked Maggie.

"I think I am okay, just sore," smiled Angelica, never letting go of Maggie.

The officers hearing what Angelica said, sprinted back to the Condo, looking to see if Brent was hiding when they noticed the Mercedes was gone.

"Crap, are we in trouble, talk about blowing a crime scene," said one of the officers.

Maggie came around about that time, walking Angelicia to the Jeep and said, "at least we got Angelica back safe. So you didn't blow it altogether."

Chapter Twenty-Six

Alan sat in his car watching the goings-on; it was like watching the keystone cops. They all went running to the back of the Condo following a dog. He was about to get out of his car to see what was happening. When he noticed a guy with a limp, come out of the Condo, get in the Mercedes, and drive off. It was somewhat funny in a weird way.

What the heck. Alan decided to follow the car and called Sgt. Nichol to inform him of what was happening.

"You got to be kidding. They let the PERP getaway?" yelled Mike.

"Yeah, but it looks like the girl may be safe," sighed Alan, *better than Cleo, he thought.*

The Mercedes drove over to Sparks to 22689 Cottage Parkway. He opened the gate, drove through shutting it before parking the car in the garage. The house looked vacant.

Alan told Mike where the suspect was located and said he would stay until officers arrived.

"Not needed for you to stay, we know who he is. He can't run too far. Douglas County still has two of his henchmen in jail, and Lyon County has two there. I imagine he is calling his attorney right now. What I want to know is, who is our mole within the Departments?"

"I will still stay," stated Alan.

Twenty minutes later, a squad car pulled up, with Sgt. Nichols leading the way. The officers walk up to the house. Mike knocks on the door, no answer. He knocks again. This time the door opened with Brent in his robe, trying to look like they woke him up. Mike reads him his rights; they cuffed him and took him to the patrol car.

Mike saluted Alan when they drove off.

Chapter Twenty-Seven

Maggie heard they arrested Brent on kidnapping charges and attempted rape; of course, he was denying it. He did have some cuts, but said he got them shaving. Brent further, said one of his men must have used the car as he was home all the time.

Angelica filed a police report, and Maggie took all the evidence she had to help the Detectives. Now it was up to the District Attorney and the courts.

The quilting club gave Angelica a farewell party, as she finished her runner, which she was going to give to her Mother.

Maggie and Nan, thanked them for all their help and, hopefully, the courts will put this guy away for years.

Angelica was up in her room playing her drum, thinking how lucky she was to beat death twice. She had loved this man, but she would get over it in time.

Angelica had been packing her stuff to go home, not that she had much, just some clothes Maggie had bought her.

She was so blessed to have been in the Sutro Tunnel for Maggie and Nan to find her. She stopped beating her drum to give Yazoo a big hug, as she was going to miss him.

Angelica's parents, Roberto and Susan, were excited about her coming home. They drove in from Elko to pick her up. They knew she would have to go back to Reno for the trial. Everyone worried about her safety as it would be months before the trial, and possibly one of Brent's henchmen would try to do her harm.

Angelica was also happy about seeing her family. She didn't realize how much she missed them. Plus, she would be glad to see her Grandpa. He was still in a home, but was getting better.

She beat on her drum and chanted the song that Walking Eagle had taught her. Life was getting better. She couldn't believe she had run away from people who truly loved her.

Maggie was glad things were settling back to normal, so was Pete. But he wondered how long normal would last around their house.

Maggie and Nan baked a cake, some cookies and made Mac and Cheese and drove it over to Bud's house. He was sitting out in his garage with Sadie. She wagged her tail when the gals walked up. Think maybe she could smell the food?

"Hey, Bud, how are you doing?"

"Great now that you are here. Do I see a chocolate cake? I haven't had a homemade cake since Edna died," stated Bud with tears in his eyes.

"Yep. We even brought some peanut butter cookies and Mac and Cheese for dinner."

Bud did a little dance and invited them into his house. His small home was comfy and very well kept. He offered them coffee as they all sat down to chat.

Maggie said, "We wanted to tell you the story of what was going on at Sutro." And Maggie proceeded to tell him about Angelica.

Bud got up and paced his small front room, "That is terrible that someone would harm a young girl, let alone put them into prostitution. " He was visibly shaken.

"The world is changing, and there are some nasty people out there, "sighed Nan petting Sadie.

"Well, we are not here to depress you, we want you to enjoy the goodies we brought and would love to have you come to dinner," stated Maggie.

"Sadie, and I would love that."

Maggie and Nan hugged him as they put their coffee cups in the dishwasher. "I will call, and we can set up a date," smiled Maggie.

As Nan and Maggie drove off, they both said, what a super friendly person and they were glad to have met him.

Chapter Twenty-Eight

Finally, Brent went to trial. He had been in jail for several months. Brent's attorney tried everything to get him released, but to no avail. The Judge said Brent was a flight risk and wouldn't let him make bail.

In fact, Fromberg was happy Brent was in jail. He didn't like Brent much, as the man could ruin Fromberg's life. He went through Brent's files and safe searching for the damaging pictures, but never found them.

Well, things don't always work out as planned. Finally, Brent went to court, and Angelica testified. It was hard on a now seventeen-year-old to sit there and be cross-examined.

Brent's attorney basically called her a liar. He said, "You made the story up as you wanted Brent for yourself. The man was kind to everyone, helping girls out, so they weren't sleeping on the street." The attorney was brutal to a juvenile and made Brent sound like a saint.

Brent denied everything and claimed Angelica made up stories about her bruises. Even though the District Attorney had pictures and police statements. Brent never took the stand, as his attorney did all the talking. The hearing lasted one week.

After the hearing was over, everyone sat in court to hear the Judge's penalty decision. Shockingly, Judge Mary Davis ruled that there wasn't enough evidence to charge Brent. She stated the District Attorney couldn't prove without a doubt Brent had beaten Angelica or that he was even there at the kidnapping scene, even with Angelica's testimony and the police report.

The Judge found him not guilty and released him. The spectators in the courtroom were dismayed, and there was an uproar. Even the press couldn't believe it. What kind of justice system do we have that a person like Brent would walk out of the courtroom a free man?

Brent knew the hearing cost him some favors but was glad it was over. He had a business to run. Plus, Brent still wanted to deal with Angelica. He was relieved that he had appeared in front of Judge Davis, as he had some good stuff on her. The Judge liked girls and teenage boys.

Brent turned as he was walking out the courtroom and looked at Angelica, pointing his finger like a gun, to say I am not done with you. Angelica turned white with fear, as she knew he or one of his henchmen would hunt her down and kill her. He wouldn't miss this time.

Maggie, Nan, and Pete were furious, as well as Angelica's folks. How could this be??? That this horrible man would walk.

Brent proceeded out of the courtroom, head held high, like a proud peacock. There was a crowd of people outside with the reporters. Loving the attention, Brent said to the reporters, "it is sad what happened to the girl, but I am innocent, and the Court did the right thing. Justice prevailed."

Brent no sooner finished talking, when a shot rang out, and Brent dropped to the steps with a bullet hole between his eyes. The crowd started screaming and running. All except for one man who held his hands up and had placed the gun on the ground. Reno Police grabbed and cuffed him immediately. The man shouted out, "Now that is justice."

Angelica couldn't believe what happened. She was free. Brent couldn't hurt her anymore. Maggie, Nan, Pete, and her parents were all thinking the same thing.

Mr. Thompson, Cleo's father, had done the world a favor. The sad part was he felt he had nothing to live for, as he had lost everything. He wanted revenge. After Cleo's death, his wife died from cancer, never getting to see her daughter again. Brent had driven their only child to commit suicide. Now justice was served.

Angelica said," I want to testify at his trial, to make people understand what a terrible man Brent was." Everyone shook their head in agreement.

Chapter Twenty-Nine

For the next year, Angelica talked about her life and how the Drum of Hope helped her through everything and is still helping. How the making of the drum taught her to cope with things she didn't have any control over.

She was growing up. Angelica will be eighteen this year and is wise beyond her age. She is going to college, planning on being a counselor for young girls who were involved in one way or another in sex trafficking. Maggie and Nan are helping the family with the college bills.

This is an article Angelica wrote for the local paper to make people aware of the growing problem.

Human Trafficking is Modern Day Slavery.

There are more slaves in the world today than at any time in history! Think about it...

Each year over two million women and children are seduced, sold or kidnapped into slavery and within the U.S. over 300,000 annually.

It all boils down to money. Human trafficking is the fastest-growing crime in the world and ranks second only to drugs as the most lucrative illegal moneymaking venture in the world.

There is such a high demand for commercial sex, and a person can be sold time after time. Until we decrease demand, more and more victims will continue to be exploited.

Watch who your kids talk to online, try to understand that they are growing up in a society that is different than when you grew up.

We tend to think this issue, as profound as it is, is a world away, and only a select few places are impacted. That couldn't be farther from the truth. This is occurring in our towns, right under our noses.

Angelica worked with people to encourage the President to sign a new executive order. This type of crime will not be solved right away, but Angelica vows to work on trying to help the victims as long as she can.

Maggie and Nan are working with her to make people aware of this type of crime. The three of them talk to any group that will listen, the Rotary, Lions Club, Chamber of Commerce, schools, etc.

Post notes from the Author

If you see something that doesn't look right regarding women and children, report it. Don't let your children walk alone or stand at a bus stop alone. Women don't park next to a van.

This isn't the same world we grew up in the 70, 80, 90, even up to 2000, so be aware.

The sad part about this type of crime is that even if the boss is found guilty, they may serve two years if that, then they are out to do it again. They have too much information on influential people who help them get away with this type of crime.

Below is the new executive order on sex trafficking from President Trump. It is lengthy, but it should cover most of the bases.

Executive Orders
Executive Order on Combating Human Trafficking and Online Child Exploitation in the United States
Law & Justice
Issued on: January 31, 2020

By the authority vested in me as President by the Constitution and the laws of the United States of America, including the Trafficking Victims Protection Act, 22 U.S.C. 7101 et seq., it is hereby ordered as follows:

Section 1. Policy.   Human trafficking is a form of modern slavery. Throughout the United States and around the world, human trafficking tears apart communities, fuels criminal activity, and threatens the national security of the United States. It's estimated that millions of individuals are trafficked around the world each year. This includes into and within the United States. As the United States continues to lead the global fight against human trafficking, we must remain relentless in resolving to eradicate it in our cities, suburbs, rural communities, tribal lands, and on our transportation networks. Human trafficking in the United States takes many forms and can involve exploitation of both adults and children for labor and sex.

Twenty-first century technology and the proliferation of the internet and mobile devices have helped facilitate the crime of child sex trafficking and other forms of child exploitation. Consequently, the number of reports to the National Center for Missing and Exploited Children of online photos and videos of children being sexually abused is at record levels.

The Federal Government is committed to preventing human trafficking and the online sexual exploitation of children. Effectively combating these crimes requires a comprehensive and coordinated response to prosecute human traffickers and individuals who sexually exploit children online, to protect and support victims of human trafficking and child exploitation, and to provide prevention education to raise awareness and help lower the incidence of human trafficking and child exploitation into, from, and within the United States.

To this end, it shall be the policy of the executive branch to prioritize its resources to vigorously prosecute offenders, to assist victims, and to provide prevention education to combat human trafficking and online sexual exploitation of children.

Sec. 2. Strengthening Federal Responsiveness to Human Trafficking. (a) The Domestic Policy Council shall commit one employee position to work on issues related to combating human trafficking occurring into, from, and within the United States and to coordinate with personnel in other components of the Executive Office of the President, including the Office of Economic Initiatives and the National Security Council, on such efforts. This position shall be filled by an employee of the executive branch detailed from the Department of Justice, the Department of Labor, the Department of Health and Human Services, the Department of Transportation, or the Department of Homeland Security.

(b)   The Secretary of State, on behalf of the President's Interagency Task Force to Monitor and Combat Trafficking in Persons, shall make available, online, a list of the Federal Government's resources to combat human trafficking, including resources to identify and report instances of human trafficking, to protect and support the victims of trafficking, and to provide public outreach and training.

(c)   The Secretary of State, the Attorney General, the Secretary of Labor, the Secretary of Health and Human Services, and the Secretary of Homeland Security shall, in coordination and consistent with applicable law:

(i)   improve methodologies of estimating the prevalence of human trafficking, including in specific sectors or regions, and monitoring the impact of anti trafficking efforts and publish such methodologies as appropriate; and

(ii) establish estimates of the prevalence of human trafficking in the United States.

Sec. 3. Prosecuting Human Traffickers and Individuals Who Exploit Children Online. (a) The Attorney General, through the Federal Enforcement Working Group, in collaboration with the Secretary of Labor and the Secretary of Homeland Security, shall:

(i) improve interagency coordination with respect to targeting traffickers, determining threat assessments, and sharing law enforcement intelligence to build on the Administration's commitment to the continued success of ongoing anti trafficking enforcement initiatives, such as the Anti-Trafficking Coordination Team and the U.S.-Mexico Bilateral Human Trafficking Enforcement Initiatives; and

(ii) coordinate activities, as appropriate, with the Task Force on Missing and Murdered American Indians and Alaska Natives as established by

Executive Order 13898 of November 26, 2019 (Establishing the Task Force on Missing and Murdered American Indians and Alaska Natives).

(b)   The Attorney General and the Secretary of Homeland Security, and other heads of executive departments and agencies as appropriate, shall, within 180 days of the date of this order, propose to the President, through the Director of the Domestic Policy Council, legislative and executive actions that would overcome information-sharing challenges and improve law enforcement's capabilities to detect in real-time the sharing of child sexual abuse material on the internet, including material referred to in Federal law as "child pornography." Overcoming these challenges would allow law enforcement officials to more efficiently identify, protect, and rescue victims of online child sexual exploitation; investigate and prosecute alleged offenders; and eliminate the child sexual abuse material online.

Sec. 4.   Protecting Victims of Human Trafficking and Child Exploitation.   (a) The Attorney General, the Secretary of Health and Human Services, and the Secretary of Homeland Security, and other heads of executive departments and agencies as appropriate, shall work together to enhance capabilities to locate children who are missing, including those who have run away from foster care and those previously in Federal custody, and are vulnerable to human trafficking and child exploitation. In doing so, such heads of executive departments and agencies, shall, as appropriate, engage social media companies; the technology industry; State, local, tribal and territorial child welfare agencies; the National Center for Missing and Exploited Children; and law enforcement at all levels.

(b) The Secretary of Health and Human Services, in consultation with the Secretary of Housing and Urban Development, shall establish an internal working group to develop and incorporate practical strategies for State, local, and tribal governments, child welfare agencies, and faith-based and other community organizations to expand housing options for victims of human trafficking.

Sec. 5. Preventing Human Trafficking and Child Exploitation Through Education Partnerships. The Attorney General and the Secretary of Homeland Security, in coordination with the Secretary of Education, shall partner with State, local, and tribal law enforcement entities to fund human trafficking and child exploitation prevention programs for our Nation's youth in schools, consistent with applicable law and available appropriations.

Sec. 6. General Provisions. (a) Nothing in this order shall be construed to impair or otherwise affect:

(i) the authority granted by law to an executive department or agency, or the head thereof; or

(ii) the functions of the Director of the Office of Management and Budget relating to budgetary, administrative, or legislative proposals.

(b) This order shall be implemented consistent with applicable law and subject to the availability of appropriations.

(c) This order is not intended to, and does not, create any right or benefit, substantive or procedural, enforceable at law or in equity by any party against the United States, its departments, agencies, or entities, its officers, employees, or agents, or any other person.

DONALD J. TRUMP
THE WHITE HOUSE,
January 31, 2020.